'I've had an overwhelming urge to do this all night,' Mark said. A tug, and the ribbon came free in his hand, and Jacinth felt the soft slide of her hair against her nape.

'Don't!' she said sharply, whirling to face him.

He was very close, laughing silently down at her, his hand still in her hair. 'Sorry,' he said, obviously unrepentant. 'I couldn't resist any longer. I've been wondering what you'd look like with your hair down.'

Dear Reader

With the worst of winter now over, are your thoughts turning to your summer holiday? But for those months in between, why not let Mills & Boon transport you to another world? This month, there's so much to choose from—bask in the magic of Mauritius or perhaps you'd prefer Paris...an ideal city for lovers! Alternatively, maybe you'd enjoy a seductive Spanish hero—featured in one of our latest Euromances and sure to set every heart pounding just that little bit faster!

The Editor

Laurey Bright has held a number of different jobs, but has never wanted to be anything but a writer. She lives in New Zealand, where she creates stories of contemporary people in love that have won her a following all over the world.

JACINTH

BY

LAUREY BRIGHT

MILLS & BOON

MILLS & BOON LIMITED
ETON HOUSE, 18-24 PARADISE ROAD
RICHMOND, SURREY TW9 1SR

*Original edition published in 1988
by Silhouette Books*

*First published in Great Britain 1994
by Mills & Boon Limited*

© Laurey Bright 1988

*Australian copyright 1994
Philippine copyright 1994
This edition 1994*

ISBN 0 263 78497 5

*Set in Times Roman 10 on 11¼ pt.
01-9405-54811 C*

Made and printed in Great Britain

COOK ISLANDS

Rarotonga

TASMAN SEA

Whangarei

Auckland

NEW ZEALAND

NORTH
ISLAND

Tasman Bay

Wellington

Cook Strait

Christchurch

SOUTH
ISLAND

PACIFIC OCEAN

N

CHAPTER ONE

JACINTH wished that Philip Rotch had chosen another time and place to propose to her.

The beer garden of a tourist hotel north of the Bay of Islands was pleasant enough. Trees planted around the edges shaded white wrought-iron tables and chairs, and there was only a handful of other people about. A couple in their forties sat quietly chatting a few tables away, and a party of young people with backpacks and healthy tans had commandeered two tables in one corner of the garden. Another man sat alone on a long, slatted seat under the trees, beyond and to one side of Philip. But the very sparseness of the customers on this weekday afternoon, just after the summer holiday season, made her more conscious of Philip's intensity as he clasped her hand tightly in his and leaned over the small space between them.

"I think I've loved you since the first moment I saw you," he said, his eyes alight with emotion and his face slightly flushed.

"Philip..." Jacinth tried to move her fingers out of his, but he took no notice. Uneasily she looked away, her glance colliding with the amused blue stare of the man on the bench a few yards away. He had a glass mug of beer in his hand and sat casually, one ankle resting on the knee of the other leg, an arm negligently thrown along the back of the seat. His hair was dark and slightly tousled; he was good-looking in a rather raffish fashion, wearing faded jeans and a denim jacket over an open-necked shirt.

"Darling," Philip said, his voice unsteady, and she wrenched her attention back to him. "You will say yes, won't you?"

The look in his eyes was frankly adoring, and Jacinth felt a familiar shrinking inside. Her facial muscles stiffened, her features becoming a beautiful, icy mask, hiding all emotion. She felt the tiny, hurried beat of a pulse in her temple, but the small sign of agitation would be invisible to any observer.

"Philip," she said, keeping her voice low, acutely aware of the stranger's eyes on them, knowing with an odd certainty that he hadn't looked away. "Philip, please . . . not now."

He gave a puzzled little laugh. "Why not now? After the past few days, and especially last night. . . ." He paused meaningfully. "You did enjoy yourself, didn't you?"

"Yes," she said hastily. "It was—it was very nice."

She knew her voice sounded cold and flat, rather than appreciative. Trying to infuse some warmth, she added, "It was lovely, really. Please don't spoil it."

"*Spoil* it?" He sounded more than disappointed. Stunned, and even outraged. "Darling, don't you know how much it meant to me? Holding you in my arms last night, feeling your response to me—you've never been quite like that before."

"I'm sorry," she said as he dropped her hand, and she instinctively shifted back in her chair, putting as much distance between them as she could. "I didn't realise that you were taking it so—so seriously." She glanced fleetingly over to the wooden seat. The man there wasn't looking at them now; he had lifted his beer mug to his lips, and as he lowered it his eyes went idly to the crowd of laughing youngsters in the corner. Why, then, did she have the feeling that he was listening to every word she and Philip said to each other?

"Of course I'm serious about you!" Philip said quite loudly, and she quelled an urge to shush him as the dark man's head swivelled and she briefly caught his eye again. There was a speculative gleam there that angered her. She was not unused to appraising looks from men; a natural blonde with a good figure and long legs could hardly avoid them. Usually she could simply ignore the universal male impulse to take a second look. But this man's blatant interest in an obviously private conversation rankled. Her habitual barriers raised themselves into place. Her eyes cool, face expressionless, she turned deliberately from him, concentrating on her companion.

"I love you," Philip was saying almost sulkily. "And last night . . . I was sure you felt the same about me. You were so passionate . . . I thought it meant as much to you as it did to me."

Inwardly she squirmed. She knew that had been a mistake. But surely . . . a few kisses in the moonlight . . . Thinking aloud, she said, "I didn't think that anyone these days regarded that sort of thing as a declaration of love."

"Well, I did!" he told her indignantly. "From *you.*"

She knew what he meant. Because she had always kept him at a distance before. They had worked together for two years, since she had joined the accountancy firm in Whangarei, New Zealand's most northern city. She hoped that, having proved her ability, she might shortly be invited to become a partner herself, and knew that Philip was doing his best to influence the senior partners in favour of it. She was grateful, not least because his championship did not depend on her attitude towards him. Almost from the first, Philip, the youngest of the partners, had clearly indicated his wish for a closer relationship, but she had consistently refused his occasional invitations. So it was generous of him to champion her cause, she thought.

Because of that unqualified support, she had at last let
him take her out a few times. She liked him, but until last
night she had never allowed him more than a brief kiss as
they said good-night.

The past few days had certainly brought them closer.
The two of them had been sent north to conduct a pre-
liminary survey of the books of a boat-building firm that
looked about to go into receivership, largely because the
owners-directors, two burly, bluff-mannered brothers
with a passion for their craft but little business know-
how, had no idea of how to keep accounts. On their last
evening, Philip had suggested he and Jacinth should treat
themselves to dinner and dancing at one of the north's
most elegant tourist spots. They would be returning to the
office in Whangarei the following day, after a final
meeting with the directors of Bayside Boats. He was
pleased with the way they had worked together, both enjoying the challenge, their minds attuned to bringing
some kind of understanding to the chaos that had con-
fronted them. They had even worked into the night, and
in a place where most people were either holidaying or
catering to the holiday trade, it seemed fair to allow
themselves a little light enjoyment before returning home.

It had been a very pleasant evening. Although she
didn't do it very often, Jacinth enjoyed dancing, and the
music and the food had both been extremely good. Philip
had ordered an excellent wine to accompany their meal,
and afterwards had persuaded her to try his favourite
liqueur.

Perhaps influenced a little by the alcohol she had consumed, and by a starry subtropical night and the moonlight shining on the sea, Jacinth had been feeling more
relaxed than usual. With little hesitation she had agreed
to a stroll along the beach near the hotel where they had
rooms paid for by the firm, and when Philip took her into
his arms she had done her best to respond to his not-

unpleasant lovemaking. She had linked her arms about his neck and for the first time parted her lips and tried to kiss him back. They had stayed there for some time, and she had not even objected when his hands began to rove tentatively over her body.

She must have given a better impression of returning his ardour than she had realised, she reflected guiltily. Certainly Philip seemed to have no idea that she had felt only a mild enjoyment of his quite practised caresses, and a desire to give him pleasure because she liked him and because his eagerness aroused in her a kind of tender pity.

Deep down she was aware that there had been another, more complicated reason, too, but she wouldn't let the half-conscious thought surface.

Her refusal to let him join her in her room when they reached the hotel had been accepted with a rueful laugh. "It's probably for the best," he admitted. "I know you're not the kind to go into something like this lightly, and for the firm's sake, I suppose we ought to be careful. But—" he had lifted her hand and kissed it, a gesture she couldn't help but find touching "—I'll see you tomorrow, darling. We must talk."

Yes, they must, she'd agreed silently as she closed the door on him. Even then, she had an uneasy feeling that she might have been a little stupid. And possibly unfair.

In the morning, she told herself they had both drunk rather more wine than was wise. If Philip thought that he had moved towards an affair with her, she would soon disabuse him of that notion, and they could return to their old casually friendly footing.

She certainly had not anticipated a proposal of marriage, delivered over the drinks Philip had suggested they could do with after the meeting, which had been unexpectedly protracted and involved. They had broken for a lunch of sandwiches and coffee, but it was almost three by the time she and Philip had collected up a box of ac-

count books and untidy files of receipts and invoices to
take to Whangarei with them for detailed examination,
and made their way back to Philip's car.

She should have refused the drink and insisted on
driving straight to Whangarei, but it had seemed like a
good idea at the time....

The man on the bench put down his empty glass and
stood, thrusting his thumbs into the pockets of his jeans.
Standing, he was taller than she would have thought. His
shoulders looked very broad under the denim jacket. He
was, she supposed rather cynically, a fine figure of a man
altogether. And self-confident with it. He was looking at
her now with unabashed curiosity as he walked nearer to
their table. She stared back at him, her eyes cool and very
green.

Philip, apparently oblivious to anyone but themselves, said urgently, *"Jacinth..."*

Before she looked away, she saw the flicker of expression on the dark man's face. His eyebrows moved frac-
tionally upward, and his eyes held hers a second longer,
a wordless comment that said, "So that's your name."

And she resented it, as though he had taken something from her that she had not had any intention of giving him.

Irritation coloured her voice as she wrenched her gaze
back to the man opposite her. "Philip, I don't think this
is the right time...."

She kept her eyes fixed on Philip, but as the dark man
passed their table she *felt* that he was still studying them
both, turning his head to get a good look at Philip, taking in the angrily miserable expression on his face.

"It wouldn't matter, if you loved me," Philip said.
"Am I to understand you've just been playing around,
after all?"

She glanced behind her, saw the man opening the door
into the interior of the hotel.

"Will you *look* at me?" Philip said loudly. "Or is any passing male more interesting than I am?"

He looked past her, casting an unmistakable glare over her shoulder. Jacinth hoped the other man hadn't heard, but he wasn't that far away, and she had a feeling that his hearing was pretty acute.

"I'm sorry, Philip," she said, her voice very even in spite of her annoyance at the accusation. "It's just that he's been sitting over there listening to us for some time. It was . . . embarrassing."

"Listening? Surely you're imagining things."

"No. He's been deriving a good deal of amusement out of the situation, I'm very sure of that."

Philip started to get to his feet. "Why, the nosy—"

"Oh, do sit down!" Jacinth said sharply. "If you hadn't chosen such a public place—"

"I'm sorry." He subsided stiffly into the chair. "I didn't mean to embarrass you. I thought—I hoped—that you'd be too thrilled and delighted for it to matter. Stupid of me."

"Of course it wasn't." She was afraid her exasperation was showing. She tried to force an appropriate expression of contrition onto her face, but the muscles seemed set. "Honestly, I'm flattered, but I hadn't expected—I didn't know how you felt."

He said, "Am I going too fast for you, darling, is that it? Look, I tell you what, we'll just let it ride for now, OK? Think about it."

But she knew, starkly, that it wouldn't matter how much she thought about it, her answer would be the same. It wouldn't be any kinder to keep him dangling. "I can't marry you, Philip. I don't think I'll ever get married."

"Darling . . ."

"And please *don't call me that*." She couldn't help it, she didn't want him laying any sort of claim to her. All of a sudden, she really didn't want to be with him at all. And it was her own fault. She should never have tried to respond to him last night, feigning something she didn't really feel. "I'm going to the Ladies'," she said, getting up. "I'll meet you at the car."

After the brightness of the garden, it was unexpectedly dim in the deserted lounge. She turned into a narrow corridor, following an arrow pointing the way to the toilet facilities, and came up against a dark, bulky shape, stopping just in time to avoid a collision. They were very close, her face only inches from the open collar of the man's shirt, where a pulse beat evenly at the base of his brown throat.

She smelled clean denim and soap, the tang of beer and an indefinable personal masculine scent, and knew, before she instinctively lifted her eyes, who it was.

His face was shadowed, all dark planes and angles, but his eyes were penetrating, although the pupils were enlarged in the dimness, nearly obliterating the vivid blue irises. Jacinth's temples throbbed almost painfully, and the corridor seemed airless, forcing her to draw a quick little extra breath.

For a moment neither of them moved. Then he said laconically, "Sorry," and stepped aside, his back against the wall. As she passed him, putting out a hand to push at the swing door just ahead, he added very quietly, "Jacinth."

She didn't look round. The door swung behind her and she crossed the carpeted space to a gilded mirror hanging over a long counter. Automatically she took her make-up purse from her shoulder bag and found a lipstick and comb. Her hair was still perfectly smooth, drawn back from the symmetrical oval of her face and fastened neatly at her nape by a carved kauri clasp. She took the cap off the lipstick and rather unnecessarily re-

coloured her mouth, annoyed that her hand was not quite
steady.

Well, it wasn't every day a girl got a proposal of marriage.

She put the cap back on and returned the lipstick and
the unused comb to her bag, smoothed her beige linen
skirt and tucked the short-sleeved red cotton blouse more
firmly into the waistband. Checking her appearance
again in the mirror, she stopped for a moment to stare at
herself. Her face looked composed and slightly withdrawn, but her eyes were brilliantly green, and there was
a faint pink colour under the pale golden tan on her
cheeks. She didn't want to admit that it had been put
there by the inflection in a stranger's deep voice, calling
her softly by her name.

CHAPTER TWO

"I've cooked veal escalopes for you," Nadine Norwood said. "To celebrate your homecoming."

Jacinth, taking a flowered china bowl of potatoes from her mother to place it on the dinner table, smiled and mildly protested, "I've only been away a few days. But thanks, anyway. I know I'll enjoy it."

"Of course you will. How is Philip?"

For just a moment, Jacinth hesitated. "He's fine," she said lightly. Actually, he had been showing every sign of being deeply depressed when they arrived back at the office but she sincerely hoped that he would get over that, and she didn't want to have to answer too many questions. As her mother discarded the frilled apron tied about her tiny waist, Jacinth took a chair and waited for Nadine to join her.

"He's very interested in you," Nadine said, casting her an arch look as she sat down. "I shouldn't be surprised if he proposes to you, soon."

Jacinth felt her lips compress slightly. Picking up a heavy silver spoon, she helped herself to potatoes. Her mother looked at her sharply. "Or has he already?" she said, her blue eyes inquisitive. She was a very pretty woman, the fair hair, which her daughter had inherited, permed into a fluffy halo about a truly heart-shaped face. She looked ten years younger than her actual age, with a trim, petite figure to match her youthful face.

Jacinth carefully replaced the silver spoon, and her mother put a hand on her arm and said playfully, "Oh, go on, darling, you can tell me! He has, hasn't he?"

Jacinth sighed. Nadine would just keep on until she either confirmed or denied, and she didn't suppose it was much use denying it.

"Yes," she said briefly. "Do you want some peas?"

Hopefully, she passed the dish to her mother, but Nadine wasn't easily sidetracked. "I knew it!" she said, clasping her hands and casting her eyes heavenward, as though in prayerful thanks. "Three days alone with you, and he couldn't resist you."

"Mother—"

"Oh, darling, please don't say 'Mother' to me in that awful, *long-suffering* way!" Nadine wrinkled her nose, smiling prettily. "You make me feel so old!"

"I'm sorry," Jacinth said automatically.

"Well," Nadine patted her arm in forgiveness, "tell me all about it."

I won't! Jacinth thought in a sudden flash of rebellion. Then, ashamed of herself, she said, "He asked me to marry him. I turned him down."

"Turned him down?"

"Yes." She looked at her mother then, surprising a strange expression on her face. "What did you think I would do?"

Nadine smiled. "Dearest, how should I know? You've always been quite exasperatingly closemouthed about your little romances. Still, I should have thought Philip would be quite a good—"

"Catch?" Jacinth asked ironically. "I earn almost as much as he does, you know. If they make me a partner, it'll be even closer."

"A good match for you, I was *going* to say. After all, you have a lot in common. Both accountants—where on earth you got that from, I don't know, certainly not me, and your father, of course, could never keep a dollar in his pocket. You do seem to get on well together, and

Philip's not bad looking. After all, you're twenty-six next birthday, and if you don't get married soon..."

Jacinth laughed. "I'll be left on the shelf? It's all right with me. I think I can be quite comfortable there."

"Oh, darling, I can't believe that! Such a waste. You're a pretty girl—almost beautiful, in fact. And you have developed a wonderful dress sense—that understated look suits tall girls. It's wise of you to realise you could never wear the kinds of things that I do. Although I do think you could make more of your lovely hair."

"Do you want me off your hands?"

"Of course not. I'd miss you dreadfully, you know that, but I won't stand in your way. Every girl wants to get married, eventually. I hope I'll never be one of those awful mothers who won't allow their daughters to be happy." She paused, her blue eyes widening. "You didn't refuse poor Philip for *my* sake, did you?"

"No, of course I didn't. For his own, really. I don't think I'd make him much of a wife."

"What nonsense, darling. Any man would be delighted to have you grace his home."

Jacinth cast her a curious glance. For someone who prided herself on her youthful outlook, Nadine had some decidedly dated ideas. Her view of marriage and the relationship between the sexes was strictly traditional: it was the woman's job to be decorative and useful in the domestic arts, and the man's to make the decisions and shelter his woman from the winds of adversity, especially financial ones.

Jacinth didn't remember her own father, who had left them when she was barely four, except for memory flashes of someone big and smiling, but she vividly recalled a series of men who had briefly entered her mother's life since then, on whom Nadine had determinedly leaned for a time, only to find that they were broken reeds, in one way or another. Whether any of them had actually been her mother's lovers, Jacinth didn't know. Nadine had a well-developed sense of delicacy, and would never have allowed such a relationship to become overt in the presence of her daughter. But that the men had been attracted to her mother's blond prettiness and air of helpless femininity, she had no doubt. Her mother sparkled in the company of a personable male of any age. When Jacinth herself had started dating in her teenage years, she well remembered the skilful and apparently unconscious ease with which her mother had fascinated her young escorts.

Jacinth, never a chatterer, had been left more tongue-tied than ever while her mother took over the conversation, and when Nadine gently chided her afterwards for not putting the boys at ease—"After all, dear, in your home, it's up to you to make them feel comfortable, you should at least make an *effort*"—she simply shrugged and said, "Well, they'd rather talk to you anyway." Nadine knew all the latest pop songs and the hottest film stars, and talked to the boys, as she said, "on their own level". They were, to a man, impressed by her.

When Jacinth said so, Nadine would laugh delightedly, and say, "Oh, well, at your age, I suppose I was awkward with boys, too."

Jacinth couldn't imagine it. Nadine, she thought, had always been conscious of her own power over the other sex, and known how to exercise it.

It wasn't a power that lasted, though. The broken reeds had their own revenge, and Jacinth remembered the storms of tears that had accompanied Nadine's discovery of their imperfections. Sometimes there had been raised voices and slammed doors, followed by bouts of hysterical weeping on Nadine's part that left her drained and puffy-eyed, and Jacinth indignant and upset as she tried to comfort her mother.

"You can't trust men," Nadine would say resentfully, dabbing at her swollen eyes. "They're all the same, out for what they can get." But within months, she would have another man in tow, calling at the house, taking her out, bringing flowers, doing her income tax forms for her, and mowing her lawn. This one, she was always convinced, was different, and she would be happily aglow, bubbling with life and full of extravagant plans. Until the next disastrous break-up.

By the time she was thirteen, Jacinth had formed her own opinion of men, unconsciously coloured by her mother's long and fruitless search for one she could rely on, and her repeated disillusionments. A year or two later, Jacinth herself was dating, out of curiosity and a natural desire to be like the other girls her age. But although she liked some of the boys who asked her out, she was repelled when they pressed hot lips to hers and clumsily fumbled at her body. When they drifted off to other girls, she wasn't surprised. That men were fickle she knew from her mother's experience, and she didn't particularly care when one of her girlfriends told her indignantly that the rumour among the boys was that Jacinth was frigid. She merely shrugged and said, "Maybe it's true."

At school she threw herself into her studies, winning a scholarship to university and choosing to study accountancy, because she had a flair for figures, liked the neat predictability and precision of mathematical calculation, and found the business world a fascinating study. And because a career in accountancy promised security and independence.

As she grew older and the men who asked her out were more experienced, she found their caresses less repugnant, but was still convinced that she had a low sex drive. Once or twice she had been tempted to give in to some man's insistent lovemaking, to find out if she was really frigid. But if she liked the man, it didn't seem fair to use him as some kind of experimental subject, and if she found that she didn't like him so much after all, she couldn't bring herself to allow him such intimacy with her. Particularly after she realised that for a certain type of man her apparent self-sufficiency, the cool exterior that she had developed as a defence against hurt, was a challenge; that for them an affair would be less a relationship than a conquest. And always there was a wariness engendered by the knowledge of the emotional seesaw her mother seemed to have lived on for most of her life.

"I'm going to hand over the Bayside Boats account to you, Jacinth," Philip told her the next morning. He was shuffling papers on his desk, his voice efficient and impersonal. "Can you clear your desk of everything else for a couple of weeks, do you think?"

"I'd like to take one more day to finish the Caswell accounts," Jacinth told him. "I've nearly got them wrapped up, and I have an appointment to see Mr. Caswell this afternoon."

"Yes, fine. What about lunch with me?"

Her heart sank a little. "I am very busy. If I'm to get Mr. Caswell's books ready for him by two..."

He looked up at her then. "Please!"

"Philip—"

"I must talk to you, Jacinth."

As she still hesitated, he said hurriedly, "All right, then. Some time over the weekend. Would that be better?"

At least it would be more private, she thought. "Do you really think there's any point in us seeing each other any more?" she asked him. "Outside working hours, I mean."

"I still hope you'll change your mind, you know."

"Philip, I've told you—"

"I'll pick you up Saturday morning," he said, suddenly masterful. "And I promise I won't try to push." He smiled at her, and she gave in, defeated. He was a nice man, and she didn't want to hurt him. But she would have to make it clear to him on Saturday that there was no chance of her changing her mind. The look in his eyes belied his studiedly casual manner, making her feel guilty and upset, and she left as quickly as she could, hiding a sense of shrinking distaste behind a calm, aloof expression. Too late, she wished she had never let their relationship become personal.

She crossed the reception area quickly to her office without looking at anyone, vaguely aware of someone coming in the glass doors from the street and stopping at the reception desk.

She had scarcely begun work when the intercom on her desk buzzed. "Miss Norwood, there's a Mr. Harding to see you."

The name was unfamiliar. "I don't have any appointments this morning," Jacinth said.

"No, he doesn't have an appointment, but Mr. Rotch said would you see him, please. It's something to do with Bayside Boats."

A creditor? she wondered. When a firm was in financial trouble, word got around fast. Well, there wasn't much she could say at this stage, and certainly she wasn't about to divulge any of her clients' business without authorisation. He might have made an appointment, she thought, rather annoyed. But if Philip wanted her to see the man...

"All right," she said. "You'd better send him in."

When the door opened she looked up and for a moment didn't react at all. Then she shot to her feet, and barely stopped herself from blurting out, What are *you* doing here?

Because it was the man from the hotel garden.

In half a second she had controlled her sense of shock, and managed to say quite calmly, "Mr. Harding?"

He closed the door carefully before he said, "Yes. Miss Norwood."

Jacinth swallowed, and put on her most professional manner. "Please sit down."

As she sank into her chair he took the one opposite that matched it, grey wool a couple of shades darker than the carpet. He surveyed her across the black leather of her wide desk, the blue eyes just as speculative but less amused than yesterday. He was wearing an open-necked shirt again, this time with jean-cut trousers and no jacket. He didn't seem to share her surprise, but then, he had probably seen her as she left Philip's office, when he was coming in the door. She didn't think for a moment that he had failed to recognise her. Strangely, she experienced again the claustrophobic sensation that had assailed her when they had almost collided in the hotel corridor. Something fluttered in her throat, and she had to take a moment to quell the odd, unreasonable feeling of fright.

"What can I do for you?" she enquired, coolly polite.

"You can tell me what's going on at Bayside Boats."

Her lips compressed. "I don't think so," she said crisply. "The directors—"

"I've spoken to Ted and Oscar," he said, "yesterday. They tell me that you people advised them to refer all queries to you." He slid a hand into his pocket and produced an envelope. "Perhaps this will help."

He tossed the envelope on the desk, and she picked it up. The single sheet of paper inside asked her to tell Mr. Mark Harding whatever she felt he should know about the financial affairs of Bayside Boats. It was signed by the directors. She wondered how he had got it out of them. But that thought was ridiculous, she realised. There was

nothing remotely threatening about the man, although he
wasn't, obviously, the type to be pushed around. There
was absolutely no reason for her mental warning signals
to be running riot as they were.

Carefully she folded the letter and slipped it back into
its envelope, reluctant to look at Mark Harding again.
When she did, it was with delicately raised brows. "What
is your interest in Bayside Boats, Mr. Harding?"

"They're doing some work for Pacific Trade
Enterprises. I'm the director of PTE."

"The managing director?"

He hesitated, then confirmed it. "Yes."

Jacinth had never heard of the firm, and it crossed her
mind that he didn't look like a managing director of
anything; apart from the way he dressed, he couldn't
have been more than thirty-five at the most, probably
he'd be thirty-two or three. She said politely, "I see."

"I don't know if you do," Mark Harding said. "The
people at Bayside said that your firm advised them to
suspend work on projects for which they don't have the
materials in hand."

"That's correct."

"They have a schooner half finished for us, and if it's
not completed by the contract date—"

"Mr. Harding, I'm afraid I'm not able to go into details at this stage, but I can assure you that everything
possible will be done to meet all existing contracts." The
fact was, Bayside didn't have the cash to buy any more
materials, and their suppliers were refusing them credit,
but she wasn't ready to tell anyone that, yet. It wouldn't
have been in her clients' interests, she was sure.

"If they're closed down—"

"We are trying to avoid that, Mr. Harding."

"So tell me, what exactly are you going to do?"

"We are going to advise our clients, of course—"

Impatiently, he stood up, to lean his hands on her desk.
"Look, Miss Norwood, I realise this doesn't mean a lot
to you, but our schooner has to be in service by a spe-
cific date, otherwise several thousand cases of bananas
are going to rot in their home ports on various small islands in the Cook group, instead of being sold on the
New Zealand market. Have you any idea what that
means?"

"I suppose it means your company will lose some of its
profit, Mr. Harding, but I'm sure you understand that
our clients' interests come first. Those interests may well
coincide with yours, but it's too early to say. We'll do our
best, as I said, to help the firm honour existing contracts, but it's impossible as yet to detail exactly what arrangements will be necessary—"

Curtly, he said, "You're hedging, Miss Norwood. How
about some hard facts?"

"When we have assessed the position, I assure you—"

"*Listen* to me, you cold bitch!" he said, slapping a
hand on the desk and leaning closer.

His voice was low but savage, his eyes brilliant with
anger, and Jacinth blinked once, then with icy rage said,
"*I beg your pardon?*"

Surprisingly, he flushed, and straightened suddenly.
"I'm sorry," he said. "That was—uncalled for."

"Yes," she agreed, her lips barely moving. Her eyes,
wide and coldly hostile, met the blazing blue of his. The
warning signals had been right, after all. And his inexplicable rage wasn't just about this, she knew. It was
about yesterday, and what he thought of her treatment of
Philip, which was none of his business anyway. He hated
her, and they had scarcely even met.

"Do you know anything about PTE?" he asked
abruptly.

"No." She was tempted to add that having met its
managing director, she had no wish to know anything

more. With chill precision, she said, "I suggest, Mr.
Harding, that you're wasting your time—and mine. Until
I've had a good look at the books, I don't know whether
the firm will be able to go on trading or not. I do intend
to do that just as soon as possible." She stood up. "So if
you would care to call me sometime next week, I may be
able to tell you a little more...."

"And if I get out of your hair, you'll be able to get on
with it, is that what you mean?" He had controlled his
anger, but his voice was harsh.

She didn't smile. "Something like that."

"OK," he said tightly. "I'll call you." It sounded like
a threat.

"Goodbye, Mr. Harding."

He didn't answer, his eyes moving from hers and going over her in a curiously detached way, as though he
was summing her up, and not flatteringly. His mouth was
grim, his brows drawn close together. He returned his
gaze to her face, then nodded and made for the door.

In her mail the following day was a note on paper
headed "Pacific Trade Enterprises, Inc." and signed "M.
A. Harding, Director, New Zealand."

"For your interest," the note said briefly in black type.
And under the signature was a scrawled additional message: "I would appreciate your reading this. M.A.H."

"This" appeared to be a brochure about the company, enclosed with the note. There was a logo on the
front picturing a stylised palm tree and a sailing ship, and
a photograph of a couple of smiling Polynesians carrying bunches of bananas on their shoulders, with a
schooner in the background. He could appreciate as
much as he liked, Jacinth thought. She didn't have time
to read all the public relations material printed by firms
having dealings with her clients. Island economies based
on seasonal crops were vulnerable to outside factors, and

she was more concerned with the needs of the growers than with the big corporations who probably would absorb any loss quite comfortably. She would do her best for their sake, not for Mark Harding or his company. He would get what he wanted—if he was to get it at all—a lot faster if he just left her alone to go on with the job. Certainly any number of glossy brochures weren't going to ensure him special treatment.

Idly she wondered what the A in his name stood for. Mark . . . Anthony?

Her secretary asked, "Do I file this?"

"Throw it out," she answered, turning to the box on her desk that contained the material she and Philip had taken from the office of Bayside Boats. "It's not important."

On Saturday Philip arrived promptly and, after chatting for a little while to her mother, took Jacinth off in his cream Jaguar. "I thought we might go to my place for lunch," he said. "If it's all right with you."

"Yes, fine," she answered. If she had known what his plans were, she could have driven over in her own car and saved him a trip, she thought. But it was no use saying so now.

He had a pleasant town house, smaller than the old bungalow on the slopes of Mount Parahaki that she shared with her mother. It was in a quiet cul-de-sac in a new part of town, among executive-style homes.

"Drink?" he asked her as soon as he had settled her into one of the leather armchairs in his quite spacious lounge.

"Thank you."

He handed her a medium sherry from a well-stocked cabinet and poured one for himself.

At first they drank in silence; then he said, staring moodily into his glass, "It seems I took you by surprise the other day."

"Yes, you did, rather."

"I wish you'd think about it, Jacinth."

"I have. I like you very much, Philip. But—"

"Maybe I made a mistake, letting you go to bed alone that night." He looked up, and she met his eyes and shivered inwardly.

"No," she said. "No."

"You're not frightened of me, are you?"

"Of course not."

"Of sex, then?"

Jacinth shook her head. She wasn't frightened. Just strangely uninterested.

"I'd thought you might be," Philip said almost contemplatively. "I wondered, sometimes. But on the beach last week, you were so different. I figured it was just that you respect yourself too much—and I like that, Jacinth. I like a girl who doesn't sell herself cheap."

She looked at him. "I'm not in the market, Philip."

"I didn't mean that, exactly. I meant—that I admire you for valuing yourself—that I could value someone like you. I told you that I want to make you my wife."

"No, Philip, I really can't . . ."

He put down his drink with an air of decision. His eyes were very bright, his face flushed. Jacinth's fingers tightened on her glass. She felt the skin of her face go tight. Philip looked at her, then turned abruptly on his heel. "I'll see about lunch."

He served soup and a cold salad, then cheese, filling her glass with wine all the time, with a curiously watchful air. They had coffee, and afterwards she dried the dishes while he washed. She was hanging up the tea towel on its rail, her head bent, when he came up behind her, grasping her shoulder while his lips pressed at the side of her neck. When he turned her into his arms, she said, "Philip, please don't—"

"Let me make you feel the way you did on the beach that night," he said softly. "Please, Jacinth, kiss me."

His lips covered hers, smothering her protest, and for a little while she suffered his kiss, but she couldn't return it, and at last he allowed her to break away.

"Why?" he asked her angrily. "You were so sweet that one time, so—"

"Philip," she cried at last, unable to bear any more. "I was *pretending*!"

He looked stunned. "Pretending?"

Jacinth nodded. "I'm sorry. I know it was foolish of me."

"Why?"

"Because I—I like you, and I—wanted to please you. And because I hoped that—"

"That what? What did you want from me, Jacinth? Not marriage, obviously. You've turned that down."

"It's difficult to explain."

He was frowning, looking at her rather hard. "You didn't think, surely, that you needed to be nice to me to get the partnership?"

"No. I know you're not like that. It was nothing to do with the firm—or you, really."

"I don't understand. If you don't really want me— well, that's understandable, I suppose. But why bother to pretend?"

"I thought it might help me to—to feel something for you."

She moved away from him, going back to the living room. Picking up the small shoulder bag she had brought with her, she turned to face him as he followed her.

"Does that mean that you feel nothing for me?" he demanded, looking baffled and irritated.

"Liking," she said. "I suppose I'm fond of you, Philip. But that's not enough, is it?"

He shook his head. "Tell me something. Have you ever felt more than liking—for any man?"

For a moment she wanted to scream at him to mind his own business. But nothing of that showed in her face. Perhaps she owed him the truth. His ego had taken a battering, and maybe it would help if he realised he wasn't the only man who had failed to stir her emotions. She put the strap of her bag over her shoulder and said, "No. Not really."

He drove her home, and when they were nearly there he said, "Jacinth—there's something I want to say. I hope you'll try to understand. I don't think that I can take the prospect of working with you indefinitely. Not— feeling the way I do, and knowing that you—well, that you're completely indifferent. Do you think that you could—look for another partnership?"

Her first reaction was pure, frustrated rage. Oh *damn* him, *damn him*, she thought. Why did he have to fall in love with her? Why did he have to let stupid emotion rule his life—and worse, hers? Why couldn't *he* be the one to leave the firm if he couldn't bear to work with her?

"Do you think that's fair?" she asked him, keeping her voice perfectly calm, like her face.

"No, of course it isn't *fair*!" he said harshly. "It's just something I have to ask, that's all."

In a chilly little voice, she said, "Are you withdrawing your support for my partnership, then?"

He stopped the car at her gate and turned to her, and she was shocked by the hurt in his eyes. "No. Not if you insist on going for it. But I don't know how I can work alongside you, feeling the way I do."

"Surely you'll get over it!" She was unable to keep the impatience out of her voice. "It's not the end of the world!"

"You have no idea, do you?" he said, with a kind of angry contempt. He looked at her wonderingly. "You're so beautiful, but you're the original ice-maiden, Jacinth. No feelings at all. Will you just try to understand us ordinary mortals, for once? I am *dying* inside, here. If you don't go, I'll have to. That's it, OK?"

"I'm . . . I'm sorry," she whispered, instinctively moving away from him, her face freezing over. She didn't understand at all, but she could see he was suffering. "All right. I'll go. Just give me some time."

"Yes, of course," he said, closing his eyes. "All the time you need."

CHAPTER THREE

"How like a man," Nadine said bitterly. "Oh, my poor darling, what will you *do*?"

Jacinth shrugged. "Find another firm to work for."

"But the partnership!" Nadine wailed. "It was practically yours, and he's snatched it away from you. Oh, he has no right to do that to you, it's so unfair!"

Jacinth thought so, too, but her mother's reaction wasn't helping.

Nadine said suddenly, "Surely he can't make you resign? You don't have to do it."

"Philip isn't trying to *make* me do it, exactly. He hasn't made any threats or promises, just asked me very nicely if I'd mind moving on."

"But you don't *want* to!"

"I think I do, now," Jacinth said wearily. "I certainly don't think it would be very comfortable working with Philip, after this."

"Oh, you poor baby!"

"I'm not a baby, Mother. It's all right, I'll find something."

"You'll always be my baby, darling," Nadine said, her eyes misting. "After your father left, you were all I had. I don't know how I'd have coped, if I hadn't had you to think of...."

Jacinth clenched her teeth. She had heard the story so many times. How her mother, shattered by her husband's defection, had struggled bravely to keep herself and her child, with precious little help from the erratic maintenance payments her husband had made. Turning

her talent for dressmaking to good account, she had
managed to keep up the mortgage payments on the house
without having to lower herself, as she thought of it, to
depending on "government handouts," until Jacinth
began earning good money and they were able to pay off
the mortgage altogether. And the final line, "But it was
worth it, for you, darling. It was worth all the hardship
and sacrifices I made for my baby."

"I'm glad you think so," Jacinth murmured.

"And it hurts me to see *you* hurt like this."

"I'm not hurt, really," Jacinth protested. In fact, she
was more annoyed than anything, and deeply uncomfortable, but Philip was badly hurt, and she couldn't see
herself staying on in the firm, rubbing salt into his
wounds.

"Of course you are," Nadine contradicted her. "Oh,
you always try to hide your feelings, but I know my
daughter—underneath that brave face, darling, you're
just as sensitive as I am. And you know, you don't have
to hide it from *me*."

Desperately, Jacinth said, "It's getting late. Shall I peel
some potatoes for dinner?"

"Oh, there's plenty of time, but—yes, if you like."
Nadine's face lit up suddenly. "Why don't we go to the
pictures afterwards? Cheer ourselves up."

"Is there something good on?" Jacinth didn't particularly want to go out, but an evening at home was going to be a bit of a trial, she could see, with her mother
oozing sympathy from every pore. She didn't really care
what the film was.

There was a choice between a space-opera and a light
romantic comedy that had received good reviews and
starred Oscar-winning actors.

"No contest," Jacinth agreed, when her mother said
that of course they would go to the comedy. She didn't

feel like comedy, but perhaps her mother was right, they needed cheering up.

There was a patch of unseasonable mist down near the river, where yachts from all over the world rode at anchor and some fishing boats were tied up at the wharf on the town side. Jacinth switched on the car lights, although it wasn't yet dark. Crossing one of the two bridges spanning the water, she drove to a small car park near the theatre. The air was warm and pleasant, as it often was in the long summer evenings, reminding them that Northland's climate was subtropical, and Jacinth said, "It's almost a shame to be inside on a night like this."

The film was as good as it had promised to be. Afterwards Nadine, an inveterate window-shopper, lingered outside a boutique near the theatre, and when they got to the car park it was empty, except for a big blue car and Jacinth's red Sigma.

When Jacinth turned the key in the ignition, a tired gasp was all that the engine could manage.

"Oh, no!" She tried again, with the same result.

"What is it?" Nadine asked. "Try it again."

"I'll give it a rest first."

The next time, it seemed the engine was about to start, then it died again. Three men came in the entrance to the car park and went towards the blue car. Nadine turned her head to study them. Jacinth tried the starter again, and was rewarded with a resentful whine, and then dead silence.

"The battery's flat," she admitted finally. "My fault. I left the lights on."

"Oh, what a nuisance. Can you do anything?"

Jacinth shook her head. She couldn't see her mother pushing while she tried to start the engine.

"Those men—" Nadine said hopefully, brightening. "We could ask them if they'd help."

Nadine, in spite of bitter experience in the emotional field, had eternal faith in the ability of any male to deal with any mechanical problem.

"No." Jacinth shook her head. "We'll get a taxi, and in the morning I'll ask the garage to fetch the car and recharge the battery."

She removed the key and opened her door. "Come on, we might as well go."

Nadine sighed, and followed suit. As Jacinth straightened, one of the men called to her, "Trouble? Can we help?"

"It's all right, thanks."

She locked the door, and another voice said, "Miss Norwood. Good evening."

She looked up. But she hadn't needed to; she recognised the voice, her skin prickling into gooseflesh at the sound of it. Mark Harding.

He was coming towards them, followed by the other two men, neither as tall as he, one a lot older and grey haired, one considerably younger, probably in his early twenties, but all three of them with a striking family resemblance.

God preserve me from helpful males! she thought. They would accept her negligence as a bit of typical female folly, passing snidely amused glances among themselves, and insist on her getting back in the driver's seat while they pushed the car, shouting contradictory instructions to her and noisily encouraging one another until the engine caught and they were left standing in their rolled-up shirtsleeves, another example of masculine strength in triumph.

Resignedly, she said, "Hello, Mr. Harding."

"Got a problem?"

"Just a flat battery."

The youngest of the trio said eagerly, "Like a push? Or have you got a jump lead in the car, Mark?"

"Please don't trouble," Jacinth said firmly. "I'll get the garage to attend to it in the morning."

Her mother came to stand at her side, smiling at them all with an air of sweet helplessness. "It's very kind of you." Looking up at Mark Harding, she added enquiringly, "You know my daughter?"

The older man said, "Your *daughter*?"

His surprise was genuine, Jacinth knew. Except for the colour of their hair, she and her mother were totally unalike, and Nadine did look much younger than her true age. In this light she probably appeared only a few years older than Jacinth.

Nadine preened, and Jacinth, bowing to the inevitable, introduced Mark Harding. He took the hand Nadine held out to him, and turned to the other two. "My father, Lyle Harding, Mrs. Norwood. And my brother Darrel. Miss Norwood and I are business acquaintances," he explained.

Lyle Harding said, his admiring eyes on Nadine, "Are you sure we can't help?"

Nadine looked flutteringly uncertain, "Well, I don't really know...."

Jacinth said, "No, thank you."

"Oh, please!" the man said. "Let us drive you home, anyway. We can do that, can't we, Mark?"

"Yes, of course." He sounded coolly courteous, and Jacinth tried to refuse again, but his father had already put a hand under Nadine's elbow and was steering her towards the other car. And she wasn't exactly fighting all the way. When Mark Harding silently gestured to Jacinth to follow, she had no choice.

He drove, his father sitting beside him, and the two women shared the spacious back seat with Darrel Harding, the younger brother. Jacinth sat in silence while

Nadine asked if they had been at the film, too. Skilfully she elicited the information that the three of them had been having a dinner out to celebrate Darrel's homecoming from Canada, where he had been studying for a year after gaining his degree in Auckland. "Mark got the short straw," he said, "so he's driving tonight. Dad and I drank most of the wine between us."

About Jacinth's age or a couple of years younger, he seemed friendly and eager to please. Although he was talkative, Jacinth had the feeling that his self-confidence was all on the surface. Nadine, though, always brought out the best in men—at first.

It was only a five-minute journey, out of the city centre and across the bridge to Riverside Drive, then up one of the steep roads overlooking the boat harbour and the city lights. The house was old, but it had a magnificent view, and although Nadine complained of its inconvenience, Jacinth had always rather liked living up here, where the air seemed clear and more fresh.

Nadine invited the men in for coffee. Jacinth, whose heart sank at the thought, was perversely irritated when she glanced in the driver's mirror and saw the reluctance in Mark Harding's face change to resignation when his father readily accepted the invitation.

Inside, she volunteered to get coffee and biscuits for everyone, retreating to the kitchen while her mother settled the guests in the living room. But Mark Harding, to her surprise, followed her.

"What can I do?" he asked.

"Nothing, really, I can manage." It was a big, old-fashioned kitchen, but he still seemed to leave too little space for her.

"I'm sure you can," he said pleasantly. "But why not take help when it's offered?"

He wasn't just talking about the coffee, of course. She had refused help with the car, and if Nadine had not accepted so eagerly, would have refused the offer of a lift, too.

Jacinth filled the electric water jug, her back to him as he leaned against the table with his arms folded. Turning off the tap, she said, ''My mother and I are used to being independent.'' She switched on the jug.

''What happened to your father?''

''He left.'' Jacinth took a tray from its place on top of the fridge and put it on the table. Mark didn't move.

''I'm sorry,'' he said, as she opened the cupboard to get out some cups. ''I take it that was some time ago.''

''Yes, I scarcely remember him.''

Somehow she knew he hadn't taken his eyes off her. If he didn't like her—and he had made that blatantly obvious—why did he spend so much time studying her, like a specimen in a jar? she wondered resentfully.

''Your mother doesn't strike me as the independent type, particularly.''

''Appearances can be deceptive.''

''Yes,'' he said slowly. ''They certainly can.''

Something in his voice made her look at him rather sharply as she put the cups on the tray.

He moved aside. ''I know you didn't want us to come in.''

''I know *you* didn't want to come,'' she retorted, turning away again.

Obliquely, he said, ''We already had coffee at the restaurant.''

''Don't you want a cup, then?'' She opened another cupboard.

''I'll have one, to be sociable.'' He took the jar of instant coffee from her hand. ''Let me.'' He started spooning it into the cups.

Jacinth got out some biscuits, arranging them on a plate, and put sugar and milk on the tray. The jug boiled, and she carefully poured the hot water into the cups.

"I'll take the tray," he said. "You can bring the biscuits."

"Gee, thanks," she whispered under her breath. But she hadn't been wrong about his hearing. He turned his head as he reached the doorway, casting her a look of deep amusement, before he led the way out of the room. Walking four paces behind him like a traditional Japanese wife, she glared at his back and was irritated that she could find no fault with it. His hair was well cut, not too long or too short, his collar was perfectly clean, and there was no sign of dandruff on the shoulders of his jacket.

Her mother was talking animatedly to Lyle Harding, her cheeks daintily flushed, eyes bright, pretty legs neatly arranged to show off her slim ankles. Her expression was flatteringly attentive, and when she laughed at something Mr. Harding said, it was a sweet little trill. She looked elegant and ladylike, and no one could have accused her of flirting, but Lyle Harding could scarcely take his eyes off her.

Jacinth saw his elder son's glance of mildly amused surprise, before she turned her attention to Darrel and managed to spend the rest of the time talking to him.

As they stood up to go, Mark Harding said to Jacinth, "If I may talk business for a moment, Miss Norwood—"

Nadine laughed chidingly. "Oh, do call her Jacinth! I'm sure we're all friends by now."

"Are we?" he said directly to Jacinth.

She managed a stiff smile. "Of course."

His eyes said he knew it wasn't true. "I wondered if you'd read the brochure I sent you."

She kept her eyes steadily on his. "No, I'm afraid not." It was no use making excuses, and she wouldn't lie.

A flash of annoyance crossed his face. But his father was saying, "Come on, Mark, we can't keep these ladies away from their beds all night. We'd better be moving along."

"It was nice meeting you," Darrel said, giving her a boyish smile. "I hope we'll see you again."

His brother cast him an enigmatic glance, then looked back at Jacinth with a new glint in his eye that she didn't like. She was glad when they had left and the door was firmly shut behind them.

"What a nice family!" Nadine said complacently, putting a hand to her hair as she wandered back into the living room. "Lyle is really a charming man, and his sons are a credit to him. His wife died some years ago, apparently."

Jacinth looked at her with foreboding. She hadn't seen her mother so vivacious for ages. She knew the signs, and her heart sank.

"Darrel's nice."

"Yes." Nadine looked at her thoughtfully. "Mark seems quiet. He's very handsome though, isn't he?"

"I suppose so."

"Do you know what he does?"

"For a living? He's managing director of a company called Pacific Trade Enterprises."

"Oh, is that how you knew him?"

"Yes, he came into the office last week. I'll do the dishes, Mother, you get off to bed." She didn't fancy a post-mortem on the evening, and wanted to avoid the inquisitive look in her mother's eyes. The less she heard about Mark Harding and his family, the better.

CHAPTER FOUR

SHE expected to hear from Mark Harding, and she was right. He phoned her on Monday morning, sounding brusque. "Have you had time to examine those books yet?"

"I'm still in the process of doing it, Mr. Harding. I'll let you know when there's anything more I can tell you."

"You've told me nothing so far," he reminded her. "I've been talking to Ted."

"Ted?"

"Ted Brill," he said impatiently. "Of Bayside Boats. Ted and Oscar own the show."

She knew that, of course. She glanced at the electronic clock on her desk. Scarcely nine-fifteen. He hadn't lost any time. "Yes?"

"I gather they have a liquidity problem. They can't continue on the schooner until they get materials, and they haven't the cash."

That just about summed it up, she supposed. "Yes," she said again, carefully non-committal, faintly enquiring.

"I suggested that PTE pay for the materials direct. Cash, if necessary. Then they can get on with it. They asked me to clear it with you."

"Do you have the money?" she asked.

"I'll get it."

"Then I don't see any reason why you shouldn't do that, Mr. Harding."

There was a short silence, and she wondered if he was surprised. Then he said, "Right." Another pause, and he added, "I thought we were on first-name terms now."

"This is in business hours."

"I call most of my business contacts by their first names."

Of course he did, everyone did. She knew she was being unnecessarily formal, but for some reason she felt a need to keep a distance between them. "Call me what you like," she said stiffly, and heard him laugh softly.

"Now *there's* an invitation," he said.

She had walked right into that. Pointedly she said, "If that's all . . ."

"Yes," he said crisply. "Thank you, Jacinth. Goodbye."

She put down the receiver slowly and stared at it absently for a few seconds. Even over the telephone his voice started vibrations. The man did something to her equilibrium, and she didn't like it one bit.

That evening when she got home her mother said, "Do you mind fixing your own meal tonight, darling? I'm going out."

"For dinner?"

"Yes." Overcasually, Nadine said, "Lyle Harding rang me. He has tickets for a show at Forum North, and he asked me if I'd go with him. He suggested dinner first, in the restaurant."

She shouldn't have been surprised, Jacinth realised. It had been obvious the other night that Lyle was attracted to her mother, and certainly Nadine had sparkled in his company. "That's nice," she said, trying to sound interested and happy about it. "I hope you enjoy yourself."

"Well, it's a long time since I've had a real outing."

With a man, she meant. She had often been to shows with Jacinth, and sometimes with female friends. But a date was a different thing altogether. Jacinth hoped she wasn't on the way to being hurt and disillusioned yet again.

Jacinth opened the door when Lyle Harding arrived. As usual, her mother was several minutes from being ready, and Jacinth ushered him into the lounge, suggested he sit down while he waited, and offered to pour him a drink.

"No, thanks," he said. "I'll wait and have one with your mother when we get there. My son tells me you're an accountant."

"That's right," she said, leaning against the drinks cabinet, her hands thrust into the pockets of her flared linen skirt. Something about his tone told her that wasn't all Mark had said. She got the distinct impression that whatever the rest had been, it was less than complimentary.

"If you'll pardon my saying so, you don't look like an accountant."

Jacinth gave him a cool smile. "What do accountants look like?"

"Grey-haired, superior, and with a lean and hungry look," he said promptly.

She couldn't help smiling at the description. "And male?" she suggested with gentle resignation.

Comprehension showed in his face. "Sorry," he said frankly. "I guess I'm showing my age. My son tells me I must learn to move with the times. Says I'm an endangered species."

Jacinth raised her brows.

"Male chauvinist pig," Lyle explained.

Jacinth laughed. "Your son—Darrel, I presume."

"No, Mark."

"Really?"

"You sound surprised."

She was. For no particular reason, she supposed. "I hadn't thought he'd be a strong supporter of feminism," she confessed, adding hastily, "Well, of course, I hardly know him."

He looked at her rather speculatively, she thought. But before he could say anything more, her mother came into the room, becomingly flushed, and dressed in floating blue chiffon, which gave her a spurious air of fragility. Lyle stood up, smiling, and brushed aside her breathless apologies with a predictable but apparently quite sincere assurance that she had been worth waiting for.

It was the first of many dates, and Jacinth became accustomed to seeing Lyle Harding's car parked at their gate, and to hearing her mother talk about him. He ran a successful car parts business with branches in other towns in the north, but was planning to retire in a year or two, leaving his younger son in charge. "Darrel is a very clever boy," Nadine told Jacinth. "He got an engineering degree and then did a business studies diploma course in Canada. You remember he'd just got back from there when we met them, the night your car broke down."

"I remember," Jacinth said. Then, curious, she couldn't help asking, "Is Mark the dim one, then?"

Nadine looked shocked. "No, of course not. He's got a degree, too, in sociology and economics, I think Lyle said. He worked in the business for a while, but then he got interested in this other thing—Pacific Enterprises, it's called, isn't it? Well, you know all about that."

Not a lot, Jacinth thought, but she didn't want to pursue the subject of Mark Harding, so she let it pass.

She was more concerned at the moment with finding herself another job. Openings at a similar level to her present position were not thick on the ground in a city as small as Whangarei. And two factors, she felt, mitigated against her. She could give no really satisfactory reason for leaving the firm she was with, and there was still a certain amount of prejudice against employing a woman, even though no one would ever have said so to her face. She thought that a couple of prospective employers suspected she might be difficult to get along with, and one, a woman, asked her point-blank if she had suffered sexual harassment.

"Oh, no!" she said emphatically. "Nothing like that."

The woman looked doubtful. "You don't have to put up with it, you know," she said, "if that's the case. There are laws now."

"I know," Jacinth said crisply. "But really, it isn't that. I just feel I need a change. Something challenging."

It was the best excuse she had come up with, but it wasn't getting her anywhere. Probably it made her sound like a restless spirit who was just as likely to leave her next job at the drop of a hat.

To make things worse, one of the senior partners had sounded her out about a partnership, and when she firmly said she had other plans, he had looked, if anything, rather relieved.

"Not good for my ego," she told her mother ruefully that evening. "I really expected they'd at least try to persuade me."

"Never mind, dear," Nadine said. "I'm sure something will turn up."

"I may have to start looking in Auckland," Jacinth warned her. It had been on her mind for some time, but she knew that although her mother had coped before, when she was studying at university in Auckland, Nadine hated the idea of her living away from home.

"Do you think so?" Nadine said rather vaguely, making Jacinth wonder if she was really listening. Any other time Jacinth had hinted at such a thing, Nadine had been almost tearful, even while insisting bravely that of course Jacinth must do what was best for herself, and not bother about her silly old mother. After all, Nadine realised that she couldn't hold on to her darling forever, and the last thing she wanted was for her daughter to feel tied to her apron-strings.

"You could come with me," Jacinth said. "Of course, we'd get a place with a room for your sewing." The third bedroom had always been Nadine's sewing room, and Jacinth supposed she would want to continue doing it, even though she had few clients now, relying more on Jacinth's ability to support her.

"Well," Nadine said gently, "there's no hurry, surely. We'll think about it. You're not busy on Sunday evening, are you?"

"I don't think so. Why?"

"Well, Lyle has invited us both for dinner."

"Oh, I don't think—"

"I told him you'd come. I mean, you really haven't been out at all since you stopped seeing Philip, have you? It will do you good."

"Mother, you didn't tell Lyle I'm sitting in the cinders every weekend, or something, did you? If he's just being kind—"

"No, I promise you I didn't, honestly. He likes you, and—well, he'd like you to come."

"And play gooseberry?"

"No, of course not. Don't be so prickly. I didn't say we'd be the only guests, did I?"

So it was a dinner party. That was different, she supposed. But still she hesitated.

"Oh, do come," her mother coaxed. "For my sake. I want you to get to know Lyle. He's really a very sweet man."

He might be, but for some reason Jacinth had a distinct aversion to getting to know him. Some of the other men in her mother's life had been "sweet" too. A few of them had been nice to Jacinth, and she, starved for a

father's affection, had responded to their overtures with
some enthusiasm and a child's trust. But each one had
suddenly withdrawn from her life without so much as a
goodbye. In her more introspective moments, she supposed that was one reason she found it hard to respond
spontaneously to people, and especially to men. It didn't
exactly make for a sense of security.

Still, she was an adult now, not a child with a need for
a father figure. It wouldn't hurt to accept an invitation to
dinner.

It turned out to be a family party—Lyle's two sons and
Nadine's daughter. Jacinth was introduced to Lyle's part-
time housekeeper, a thin, rakish-looking, dark-eyed
woman called Mrs. McNab, who apparently didn't live
in, but was on call for special occasions in the evenings,
as well as cleaning the house and cooking an evening
meal three times a week. It seemed that Nadine had already met her, for the two women exchanged a brief
"Hallo" before Mrs. McNab retired to the kitchen to put
the finishing touches on their dinner.

The house was out of town, set in several acres of land,
overlooking a beach, and it was probably, Jacinth
guessed, about twenty years old. Architect-designed,
large and gracious, it must have been quite an eye-catcher
when it was new. There had been time for it to mellow,
and for the shrubs and trees in the garden to grow to a
respectable height and soften the architectural angles of
the design. The winding drive had led them to the door
through a patch of tall native trees that must have been
there before the house was built, and a few sheep grazed
the open space between the house and an unobstructed
view of the beach. Cabbage trees and flax grew in clumps
among more exotic flowers on either side of the wide
steps leading to a patio, and onto this the front door
opened. In the branches of a huge old puriri growing by

the fence at the side of the house, she caught a glimpse of
an ancient, dangling rope, and what looked like the re-
mains of a long-disused tree house. If Mark and Darrel
had grown up here, she thought, it must have been an
idyllic childhood.

. In the spacious lounge, furnished in a nice blend of
traditional and modern, with comfortable leather chairs
and sofas, and polished wood tables and cabinets,
Jacinth somehow found herself sitting next to Mark
Harding, who had handed her the glass of dry sherry she
had asked for. Darrel took an armchair at right angles to
them, and Nadine and Lyle shared the other sofa.

Mark seemed content to take little part in the conversation, but when Jacinth had finished her sherry and
Darrel jumped up to replenish it for her, Mark turned to
her and said, "I believe that you've sorted out Bayside's
problems."

"I wouldn't say they're all sorted yet," she replied
cautiously. "But if they're sensible and use the accounting system we've suggested for them, they should be able
to keep on building boats, and in time they'll be solvent
again."

"They seem to think that you're some sort of miracle
worker," he said dryly. "An angel of mercy, no less."
Obviously Mark had trouble picturing her in the role.

Jacinth shook her head. "They're paying for the service. They should have got themselves a good accountant much sooner. By the time they called us, it was nearly
too late."

"How good are you?"

"The firm has a fine reputation."

"I meant you, personally."

She looked at him directly, her eyes cool. "Very good."
She knew it was true. She had a flair for it, had consistently scored As at university, and she loved the work. All

of which meant she shouldn't be having as much trouble getting a new job as she was.

He sat back, the amber liquid in his glass still and level. He smiled a little, looking her over with an appraising glance.

"Don't say it," she advised him.

His eyebrows lifted. "Say what?"

"That I don't look like an accountant." She was sure it was on the tip of his tongue.

But apparently not. He shook his head. "Actually, I was thinking just the opposite."

"The opposite?" She thought of his father's description of the typical accountant and hoped their ideas didn't coincide.

"Yes," he said thoughtfully. "I must say, it doesn't surprise me a bit."

Somehow she didn't think it was a compliment and, annoyingly, he didn't seem disposed to elaborate. Well, she wasn't going to ask, she promised herself. He was playing some kind of game, and she didn't care for it. When Darrel returned with her drink, she smiled at him gratefully and didn't see the expression in Mark's suddenly narrowed eyes as he watched her.

Until dinner was served, she managed to keep up a conversation with Darrel and largely ignore his older brother. At the table, she was seated next to Darrel, at Lyle's left, while her mother and Mark were placed at the other side. Lyle was a good host, and Darrel and Nadine helped him to keep the conversation going. Jacinth did her best, but she was never as animated as her mother, lacking Nadine's mercurial personality, and Mark was apparently quieter than usual, prompting his father to ask him once if he was feeling under the weather.

"I'm fine," Mark answered. "Just having trouble getting a word in edgeways with young Darrel babbling on nineteen to the dozen."

Darrel, of course, denied it indignantly, and a good-natured verbal wrangle ensued until Lyle cut it short, saying, "Well, I have an announcement to make. Mrs. McNab—"

He nodded to the housekeeper who had just removed some of the plates, and she said, "Yes, I'll get it."

Mark caught Jacinth's eyes enquiringly, but she gave him back a blank stare. The housekeeper brought in a tray with glasses clinking on it, and a bottle of champagne, dewy from chilling. While she placed the glasses on the table, Lyle deftly removed the cork from the bottle with a small, satisfying pop. Jacinth, her heart beating suddenly fast, tried to attract her mother's eye, but Nadine, with a smile playing on her lips, was watching Lyle expectantly as he poured the bubbling liquid into the tall flutes, handing one to the housekeeper, too.

Mark put a hand round the slender stem of his glass. Jacinth felt him looking at her again, and she knew that they were both thinking the same thing. Darrel, after a surprised look about at them all, said, "Well, how long are you going to keep us in suspense, Dad?"

Lyle stood up and smiled down at Nadine, who was blushing becomingly as she smiled back. "We wanted our two families to be the first to know," Lyle said, "that this beautiful lady has consented to be my wife. I'm the happiest man in the world, and I hope that you'll all drink to our marriage—which will be as soon as I can persuade her to walk down the aisle with me." He put out his hand and Nadine placed hers in his grasp. Her smile was wider now, and full of pleased triumph.

Jacinth felt as though someone had hit her in the stomach; there was an empty feeling there. Unconsciously her eyes sought Mark's, and met them, and locked. For a moment they stared at each other; then slowly he rose to his feet, and looked at his father. "Sit down, Dad," he said. "I think it's my place to propose the toast." He glanced at Jacinth again, and paused. "We shouldn't be surprised, of course, but I think we all are. It doesn't seem long since you two met. But," he added, smiling at Jacinth's mother, "my father was never one to let the grass grow under his feet. I guess you've discovered that already, Nadine. I hope you don't mind if we call you that?"

"No, of course not!" Nadine smiled back at him. "You're a little old to call me 'Mother', after all!" she said playfully.

"Welcome to the family," he said, lifting his glass to her. "Dad is a lucky man."

"Hear, hear!" Darrel added, standing up with his own glass in his hand. Jacinth felt obliged to follow suit. She tried to smile, her facial muscles stiffening, a suffocating feeling in her throat. She should have expected it, she knew. But as Mark had said, the time seemed so short. What was it, six weeks, surely not more than seven, since her mother had met Lyle Harding? Of course a whirl-wind courtship was just her mother's style. She'd love the romanticism of it. But with so little time to get to know each other, how could they both be sure it was the right thing?

She took a gulp of the champagne and told herself they weren't married yet. There would be time for them to think about it. That remark of Lyle's had probably been just a figure of speech. Mark was looking at her, and she sat down again, making a business of replacing her glass on the table, keeping a deliberate smile on her lips, try-ing to look pleased instead of shocked and worried.

They took the rest of the champagne back to the liv-ing room, and Mark, refilling her glass, said quietly, "You don't look too thrilled about it."

"I'm just—surprised. Aren't you?"

"A bit." He glanced over at Nadine and his father, who were parrying some teasing remarks of Darrel's.

"My father's been lonely, these past few years," he said. "I'd like to see him happy again."

She thought he sounded doubtful. Was that a reflection on her mother? She sprang to Nadine's defence. "He's obviously very fond of my mother."

Mark turned back to her, his eyes definitely amused. "I'd say he's head over heels in love," he said frankly. "Wouldn't you?"

"I—don't know your father well enough to say." But certainly Lyle seemed on top of the world, and the way he looked at Nadine would have made any woman feel flattered and cared for.

"Well, I've never seen him like this," Mark admitted. "What about your mother? Does she feel the same way, do you think?"

"She's agreed to marry him, hasn't she?"

He looked at her. "You're a very cool lady, aren't you?"

Her eyelids came down, hiding the green glint of anger at the note of criticism in his voice. Her head turned slightly away from him. "We're not discussing *me*." This could be the best thing that had ever happened to her mother; Lyle seemed ideal in every way. But Mark had never seen him like this. Jacinth had seen her mother look exactly this way several times. And it never lasted.

Darrel came over, his eyes alight with mischief. "I guess this just about makes you our sister, Jacinth."

"Stepsister," Mark said. Looking at Jacinth, he added, "Do you mind?"

"It hasn't happened yet," she said, a little tartly because the idea hadn't occurred to her, and she found it distinctly jarring. To Darrel she said, her voice softening, "It'll take some getting used to."

"Come to think of it," Darrel said thoughtfully, "I'm not so sure that I want a beautiful girl for a *sister*."

"Knock it off, Darrel," Mark said rather sharply, and Darrel turned to him in surprise. "We've had enough romance for one evening, don't you think?" Mark added, his voice altering to a bantering tone.

Darrel grinned. "Sour grapes, then!" he said. "Just because *you're* too wrapped up in that so-called business of yours to notice when a pretty girl passes under your nose—"

"Less of the so-called, my lad," Mark said easily. "Pacific Trade Enterprises is a bona fide company, and we're doing very nicely, thank you."

"Dad's talking of retiring early, and taking an extended honeymoon," Darrel said. "Sure you don't want to come back into the old firm and be my partner?"

"Thanks, but no thanks. You don't need me."

Darrel shrugged. "Rather be running your charity, would you?"

Mark frowned. "I've told you before," he said, "it's not a charity."

"OK, OK!" Darrel held up his hands. "It's a—now what does the brochure say? 'A co-operative company formed with the aim of enabling Pacific peoples to manage their own economic resources.' Am I right?"

"I'm impressed," Mark said. "I didn't know you'd even read the brochure."

"I didn't buy shares without finding out where my investment was going!"

"Very wise," Mark said. "I'm sure Jacinth approves wholeheartedly."

"Jacinth?"

"She's an accountant," Mark reminded him.

"Oh, yeah—I'd forgotten."

"And don't tell her she doesn't look like one," Mark added. "She doesn't like it."

"I never said that!" Jacinth protested.

"Are you denying it?"

She shook her head.

Mark looked at his brother. "You see?"

Darrel burst out laughing. "You can't argue with him in this mood," he told Jacinth. "He always wins."

"Mark!" his father called. "Bring that bottle over here, will you? Nadine's glass is empty."

When he had left them, Jacinth said to Darrel, "You have shares in Pacific Trade Enterprises?"

"A few. The idea is that the Pacific islanders themselves hold most of the shares. Outsiders aren't allowed to have more than a certain number, so that they can't ever take control. The islanders only let other investors in because they couldn't find enough people in the islands with cash to spare when they started, to provide funds for the storage facilities and transport they had to have. And there's a nice little clause that means you can't take the money out of the islands once it's invested. The profits have to be spent there, to boost the local economy. I stopped off on the way home from Canada and spent some of my dividends."

"*Is* it a charity?"

"Oh, no, not really. I was just looking for a bite. At first, Mark and some of the islanders worked for nothing, or next to it, until it was set up. The first couple of years the whole thing ran on a shoestring budget. But now the business is self-supporting, and he's on salary as director of the New Zealand branch. I suspect at rather less than what a company director in New Zealand normally gets."

"And the company exports island produce to New Zealand?"

"And Australia. Actually, it's not a bad scheme."

"Who dreamed it up?"

"Oh, Mark, of course. Mark and a guy called Tu— short for something I can't remember. He comes from the

Cook Islands. Mark met him at university, and later they went crewing on a yacht together when Mark was on holiday from working for my father. Cruising round the Pacific. That's how it all started. Tu had the contacts over there, and Mark, with my father's help, had them here. You see, when the small islands start to export, they haven't the resources and the expertise to transport and market their goods properly, and when a big company takes that over, they lose their independence.''

"And this way they get the best of both worlds?''

"Yes. I tease Mark, but actually I admire him.''

Jacinth smiled. "I don't blame you.'' She wished she had read the brochure that Mark had sent her, instead of disposing of it so cavalierly. She would have treated his concern about the building of his schooner more seriously if she had known all this.

Mrs. McNab brought in coffee before she left for the evening. As he heaped sugar into his, Lyle said, "By the way, Mark, are you still wanting a company secretary?''

"Yes.'' Mark looked at his father alertly. "Why? Do you know someone who might be interested?''

His father smiled, glancing at Nadine. "Well, Nadine was saying that Jacinth is looking for a new job.'' He glanced at Jacinth's still, expressionless face, then back to his son. "I remember you saying that you would prefer someone with a background in accounting.''

No! Jacinth thought, everything in her shrinking from the thought. Why had her mother mentioned it?

There was a long pause, and then Nadine said, "I thought it might be nice. Jacinth is getting quite *desperate*, aren't you darling?''

Jacinth almost closed her eyes, turning her head away.

Lyle said jovially, "Keep it in the family, eh? How about it, Mark?''

Mark replaced his cup in the saucer with a small clatter. "I don't think so. It's not her sort of job, I'm afraid."

Lyle looked surprised, and Nadine said, "Oh, isn't it? I don't know much about these things, but from what Lyle said it seemed that it would be ideal."

Jacinth was about to deny it, but Mark forestalled her. "No," he said positively. "I'm sure it isn't what she's looking for at all. Our sort of company wouldn't attract someone like Jacinth."

He hadn't even given her a chance to refuse. On the slightest of evidence he thought he knew all about her— or he was just determined that she wasn't going to work for his precious company. Why didn't he come right out with it and say that he didn't want her, instead of pretending to know what *her* feelings were?

She said with determined sweetness, "Do you mean I'm overqualified for the job?"

He flicked a glance at her, his eyes hard. "Not exactly," he admitted, after a moment.

"What, then?" she challenged him, her eyes very green as they fixed on his face.

This time he held them with his, implicitly accepting the challenge. "I'm quite sure," he said, "that you have your sights set on a partnership in a major accountancy firm, within the next five years or so. You wouldn't want a sideways step at this stage into a secretaryship with a small co-operative enterprise like ours."

"Oh," she said, as though toying with the idea, "I don't know. It might be good experience. Even if it didn't pay much."

"The pay is average for that type of position," he said evenly. "Our employees are paid just the same as any other company's."

Not a charity, she remembered, but a self-supporting business.

"Anyway," Mark added brusquely, "this is all academic. You're not really interested—"

"Oh, but I am," she heard herself saying firmly. "I'm very interested. I think I'd like to apply for the job."

CHAPTER FIVE

AGAIN their eyes clashed, Jacinth's coolly green, and Mark's very blue and glinting with annoyance. Softly he said, "You *must* be desperate!" The hard light in his eyes asked, *Why?*

Darrel interrupted, laughing. "Because she wants to work with you? I'll say! Are you sure, Jacinth?"

Jacinth was still looking at Mark, held by that hard gaze. He said, "*Are* you sure, Jacinth?"

She almost shivered. His voice was still soft, and for a moment she was remembering again the dim corridor of the hotel. He had called her by her name in just that tone.

"Yes, I'm sure," she answered. Some warning voice inside her made her add quickly, "Sure that I'm interested. I—need to know a little more about the job, obviously."

"Ah." He sat back, and she saw by the expression that flickered across his face that he thought she would turn it down in the end. He said, "You'd better come and see me on Monday."

"What time?" she shot back.

Mark gave her a small, twisted smile that told her he knew the interview would be wasted. "Can you get away at eleven?"

She would take a long, late tea break. "Yes. All right."

His look was speculative. "I'll see you then. Do you know where we are?"

"I'll find it."

She and her mother left soon after that. In the car, Jacinth said, "I wish you hadn't told Lyle I was looking for a job."

"Why ever not, dear? It looks as though it's all going to work out very nicely."

Jacinth bit her lip. "You didn't tell him why, did you?"

"But of course I did. I'm going to marry, him, dear. Naturally we tell each other everything."

Inwardly Jacinth shuddered. She could only hope that Lyle wouldn't find it necessary to relate her mother's confidence to his sons.

The hope was short-lived. On Monday, she presented herself promptly at eleven in Mark's office. It was in an old building near the port, and in contrast to the discreet opulence of her present firm's premises, the floors were bare, varnished board partially covered with woven coconut palm mats. Some travel posters advertising Pacific destinations brightened the painted walls, and a large carving made of some dark, polished wood stood in one corner on a low table. A smiling Polynesian receptionist with a jaunty scarlet hibiscus in her sleek, intricately styled hair sat behind a small desk with a laminated wood-grain top. "Miss Norwood?" she said, looking up from a well-worn electric typewriter. "Mark's expecting you. He said to send you straight in."

The door to an inner office was ajar, and she tapped on it before entering.

It was a spacious room, with a pile of wooden boxes heaped up in one corner and a set of chipped and scratched khaki filing cabinets against one wall. Mark was seated at a large table that looked as though it had once graced a farm kitchen. It held a number of stacked filing trays, several bulky files, a variety of papers and a telephone. Under the table more boxes were stacked on top of one another, and she supposed he was using them instead of drawers. Darrel had said the company used to operate on a shoestring. This looked as though it had been replaced by two shoestrings.

As Jacinth entered, Mark put down a pen and said, unsmiling, "Come in. Please sit down."

The chair in front of the table was large, leather covered and slightly shabby, as though it had come from a second-hand shop. She glanced at the walls that held maps and what appeared to be the plans of a sailing ship. Following her gaze, he said, "That's our new schooner, the *Kia Orana*."

"The one Ted and Oscar are building for you?"

He nodded. "That's right." He glanced at the papers in front of him, as though reluctant to be distracted from them. "I wondered if you'd come."

"I said I would."

"Is the guy you're so anxious to get away from the one I saw you with up north?"

So Lyle had passed on the story. Looking away, she said distantly, "I don't think this is at all relevant."

Ignoring that, he said, "He didn't look the type for threats and harassment. And I'd have thought you'd deal with that sort of thing quite easily."

Inwardly Jacinth sighed with exasperation. "He hasn't threatened me," she said. "I am not being harassed. You shouldn't rely too heavily on third-hand information. It's apt to get garbled in the retelling."

Mark nodded. "Fair enough. So why don't *you* tell me the true story?"

"Because it's none of your business!" she snapped. "I want to leave my job. I need another one. You need a company secretary. I'm qualified to do it. I can supply references, if you want them."

"Did you bring any with you?"

Silently she took a long envelope from her bag and handed it to him. As he skimmed through the photocop-

ied papers, she sat erect, keeping her eyes on his down-
bent head. She wondered why he had disliked her, apparently on sight. She knew he didn't want her working
for him, and, perversely, she was all the more determined to make it impossible for him to refuse.

When he had finished reading he looked up. "These
are impressive."

All of them praised her ability, her efficiency, her re-
liability. Jacinth allowed herself a very tiny smirk of satisfaction.

And he didn't miss it. His eyes narrowed, and his voice
sounded slightly harsh as he said, "One thing—I realise
this job is a stopgap for you, while you wait for something better to turn up. But what we don't need is a fly-
by-night female whiz-kid, here today and gone tomorrow. The company needs some continuity and stability.
I'd expect you to undertake to stay with us for at least a
year."

Her eyes widened very slightly, her features a stony
mask. "You can have it in writing, if you like," she said.
"I won't leave before I've been here for one year."

He must have been disappointed, she thought with
satisfaction. But he didn't show it, merely saying,
"Right. Well, if that's clear . . . I'll tell you what the job
entails."

It was what she had expected, with some intriguing
differences from the usual. The head office was on
Rarotonga, the largest island of the Cooks, where a
board of directors entirely composed of Islanders ran the
export section. The New Zealand office run by Mark and
a small staff was responsible for importing and market-
ing. "This end is virtually a separate entity," he explained. "You'd do the books and report to the
shareholders here, and attend the directors' meetings of
the New Zealand section. Then there's a combined an-

nual general meeting, which you would attend, of course."

"It sounds interesting," she said.

"You'd probably have to work in here," he told her.

"Here?" She glanced about them. "In this room?"

It was big enough, but she was dismayed at the thought of sharing it with him. He knew it, too. A grim smile lit his eyes. "The only other space is a cubbyhole down the passageway to the warehouse space," he told her. "It's small and draughty and never gets any sun. And it's too far from my office. We need to be able to confer."

"Where—did your last company secretary work?" she asked him.

"We haven't had one until now, at this end. But the turnover is increasing. I haven't been able to keep up with the paperwork, and as we want to expand into importing island crafts as well as produce, later this year, the time seems right to appoint someone qualified."

"I see. And this is your office."

"And warehouse. We had an upstairs office in the centre of town until recently. But the rent got too expensive, and it's more convenient to have our entire operation in one place. We keep our overheads down as much as possible."

Jacinth bit back the temptation to reply, "Obviously." Instead, she silently let her eyes wander over the meagre, shabby furnishings.

"Yes," Mark said. "Not exactly the style that you're accustomed to, is it?"

He was still hoping she'd turn it down. When he stood up and said, "Well, thanks for coming, we'll let you know," she looked him straight in the eye and said calmly, "Do you think you should let your prejudices influence your judgement?"

His brows rose. "Prejudices?"

"I know you don't like me. But I can do the work—"

"I don't doubt it. With one hand tied behind your back, I should think."

"And I won't go back on my word," she promised.

"No," he said slowly. "I don't think that you would."

It had to mean something, she told herself. "Well then . . ."

He nodded thoughtfully. "As I said, we'll let you know."

When he phoned two days later to tell her that she had the job, she was surprised, slightly triumphant, and suddenly rather dismayed, wondering what she had let herself in for, working with Mark Harding.

"When can you start?" he asked her.

"I'm supposed to give a month's notice. But I think they might let me off with two weeks'."

"Try," he advised her. "You'll have a bit of a backlog to catch up on when you start."

That was something of an understatement, she thought when she was presented with the books on her first day with Pacific Trade Enterprises. The accounts, as far as they went, were well kept and perfectly legible, but they were not up to date, and Mark handed over a box of invoices, receipts and miscellaneous pieces of paper with obvious relief. "I haven't had time to do much about them lately," he said. "And Rosa is a good typist, and an intelligent girl, but no great shakes at figures."

Rosa was the typist-receptionist. She seemed friendly and efficient, and today the hibiscus in her hair was yellow, matching the skirt she wore with a frilly white cotton blouse.

"Was it difficult, leaving with only two weeks' notice?" Mark asked casually.

"Not terribly." Philip, who should have been pleased, had seemed more put out than the other partners, who had expressed their disappointment that she was leaving, but wished her success in her new job and farewelled her with a special afternoon tea and a bouquet of flowers. He had come into her office late in the afternoon when she was clearing her drawers, and asked if she needed help carrying things to her car.

She hadn't very much—a few books, some spare make-up and a box of tissues—and she had brought a capacious bag to put them in. "No, thanks," she said. "I can manage. Goodbye Philip. It's been nice working with you."

"Is that all you can say?" he burst out.

Her nerves tightened. "What else is there to say?"

"God, you're a cold bitch!"

That was twice she'd been called that in the space of a few weeks. And it wasn't fair. Her stomach was churning, and she felt a surge of guilty compassion for him, but her surface calm didn't crack. "Excuse me," she said, trying to walk past him, the heavy bag in her hand.

He grabbed at her, groaning, "I'm sorry, Jacinth, I didn't mean that!" and pressed a long, desperate kiss on her lips, which she suffered without moving. If it made him feel better, she didn't mind.

Afterwards, though, when she had put the bag in her car and slid into the driver's seat, she sat for a minute, taking deep breaths to relax the tension that gripped her. The kiss had been nothing to her, but some of the strength of Philip's emotion had communicated itself, and she couldn't help feeling agitated and sick with guilt, even though she was somehow incapable of showing it. Far from inflaming her to passion, he had made her freeze with distaste. And yet he was handsome and attractive and most women would probably have welcomed his kisses. Undoubtedly, there was something wrong with her.

But she wasn't telling any of this to Mark Harding. "They didn't mind too much," she said. "I had told them a few weeks ago that I might be leaving."

He said absently, "Good. Well, I'll let you get on with it. If you have any questions, I'm right over there."

A desk had been placed at right angles to his, against a wall. It had deep drawers and a good, wide top, and when he asked if it was suitable, she said it was quite adequate, thank you. The desk wasn't new, but the upholstered adjustable chair in front of it was. Mark said, "We don't want our people suffering from back problems. A decent chair is important for an office worker. I hope it's comfortable."

It was, perfectly. And the light falling from a high window across her desk made the angled lamp standing on it unnecessary at the moment. Evidently, although running on a limited budget, he had his priorities right.

He was surprisingly easy to work with, she found. He explained what she needed to know clearly and succinctly, and was patient when at first she had to interrupt his work with queries. Rosa and the half-dozen other staff, mostly concerned with the shipping and warehousing side of the business, obviously thought a lot of him. They all called him by his first name, and a friendly atmosphere prevailed not only in the lunchroom shared by all the staff, but throughout the building. He could be impatient, though, with slackness and sloppy work. She was quite sorry for a crestfallen young warehouse clerk who had been called into Mark's office to explain his failure to write up the paperwork when a load of grated coconut was taken from the warehouse for delivery to Auckland. Mark had asked her to leave them for a few minutes, and when she came back into the room, he said, "Sorry about that. I didn't want to have to tell him off in front of a witness."

"It's all right." She hesitated. "What did you say to him?"

"Nothing much. He won't be so careless a second time, though."

He looked rather grim, and she thought, I'll bet he won't. She had seen glimpses of Mark's temper.

They had not discussed anything but office matters before, but now, instead of picking up the pen on his desk, he said, as she pulled out her chair, "Has your mother said anything about her wedding plans?"

She turned to look at him, her hand on the chair back. "Yes, actually." Her mother had talked of it last night, giving a date less than a month away, and insisting that she wanted Jacinth to attend her.

Surprised and dismayed, Jacinth had said, "You mean—be a bridesmaid?"

"Well—yes. It would be so nice, darling. I won't be wearing white, of course, this time, but perhaps a rich cream satin or lace—not brocade, it's so *aging*! And too heavy for my figure. I thought turquoise for you. Lace, perhaps—although velvet would be nice. It will be cool enough for velvet by then."

"Isn't it a bit soon?" Jacinth asked. "I mean, you've only known Lyle a couple of months."

"Dear, we're both adults and we know what we're doing. As Lyle says, once we've made up our minds, what's the point of delaying? You can stay in this house, of course. I don't want to sell it, and I'll be living in Lyle's home. He's quite well-off. And generous, too. I don't need money of my own. Will you be nervous?"

"No," Jacinth answered, brushing the question aside. "But are you sure this is what you want? I mean, this isn't the first time . . ."

"Oh, really, Jacinth! Just because I made a horrible mistake marrying your father, it doesn't mean I can't have a perfectly happy second marriage. I was too young, unfortunately, to know any better then. Heaven knows, I've waited long enough for a little happiness of my own. I've devoted twenty years of my life to you. You're not jealous, are you, dear? I suppose it's natural, but really, Jacinth, you're old enough to stand on your own feet now, you know."

Jacinth blinked, taken aback. "Of course I'm not jealous!"

"Well, perhaps not consciously." Nadine patted her cheek lightly. "But maybe, deep down, you're a little afraid of losing your mummy, hmm? Don't worry, my darling, I'll always love you, of course I will. And Lyle, bless him, will welcome you in our home. He's taken quite a fancy to you—the daughter he never had. So—you will be my bridesmaid, won't you, dear—with a generous heart?"

Jacinth, stifling her misgivings, gave in. The date had been set, and there was nothing more she could say.

Now Mark was saying, "Apparently it's going to be you and me—supporting our parents on the big day."

"Oh. You mean, you're going to be your father's best man?"

He nodded. "I believe it was your mother's idea."

Probably, Jacinth thought. But she didn't care for the slightly dry note in his voice. "I expect they both would like their children to take part in the ceremony," she said. "What about Darrel? Will he feel left out?"

"He's been designated usher, haven't you heard? How big is this wedding going to be, do you know?"

Jacinth shook her head. She hadn't expected it to be big enough to need ushers. Her mother had few close friends, and no more than intermittent contact with the couple of aunts and some cousins who were the only relatives that Jacinth knew of. "There'll be very few people from my mother's side," she said positively.

Mark looked at her thoughtfully. "My father has a lot of friends."

"Well, if he wants to invite them all, that's his business, isn't it?"

Mark raised his brows. "Did I say otherwise?"

There was a double knock on the door, and Darrel came into the room. "Hi, you two," he said. "How's the banana business?"

"We do deal in other things," his brother said mildly. "What do you want?"

"Actually, I want to take Jacinth out for lunch. Haven't seen her since Dad made his big announcement, and I thought it was time I got to know my sister-to-be. You can come, too, if you like," he added to Mark.

Mark didn't look a bit pleased. He hesitated before saying, "No, thanks. I'm rather pressed for time at the moment. You two go ahead and enjoy yourselves."

Jacinth might have turned down the invitation, but she didn't want to dampen Darrel's high spirits, and somehow the fact that Mark didn't approve made her want to go, anyway.

Darrel was entertaining and uncomplicated, and she felt relaxed in his company. She didn't feel at all relaxed with Mark. Their working relationship seemed smooth enough, but there was a cool wariness between them, a tension that she was always uneasily aware of. Mark didn't joke with her as he did with the other members of his staff, didn't smile at her the way he did at Rosa when they talked, or notice what she wore. She had heard him tell Rosa that a particular dress suited her, or that a pretty new blouse looked good, or that he liked the colour of the flower in her hair. He never gave Jacinth an appreciative glance, although occasionally she felt his eyes on her with an air more of critical appraisal than approval, which reminded her of the first time she had seen him.

He looked that way again when she came back from
lunch with his brother, glancing up from the papers on
his desk, his eyes sharp and probing.

It made her feel oddly defensive, and she said in
slightly brittle tones, "I'm not late, am I?"

"No." He paused, still looking at her in that disconcerting way. "Enjoy yourself?"

"Yes. You told me to."

His mouth curved satirically. "It wasn't an instruc-
tion."

She crossed to her desk and bent to place her bag in the
bottom drawer. Straightening, she saw that he was still
looking at her. Irritably, she decided to confront him
head-on. "Is something wrong?" she asked innocently.

"There's never anything wrong with you, Jacinth."
His eyes lowered over her, slowly but impersonally taking in the trim, belted navy frock with the white shirt
collar and slim skirt, the sheer stockings and navy blue
high-heeled shoes. "Never a hair out of place, never a
smudge on that perfect nose, not a crooked hem or a
loose thread in sight."

"Somehow," she said, "that doesn't sound like a
compliment. Why don't you like me, Mark?"

Something flickered in his eyes. "You shouldn't jump
to conclusions."

But he wasn't denying it. "It's true," she said flatly.
"And I've never done anything to you. Have I?" She
dared him to answer, her eyes challenging, slightly
scornful.

"Not a thing," he agreed softly, a peculiar smile playing about his mouth. "All you've ever done is—be you."

Which told her something, she supposed. Surprisingly,
she was hurt. It shouldn't have mattered, but it did, and
she looked away from him, her eyelids drooping, and
went to her desk, relieved when Rosa opened the door

and came in with a sheaf of letters in her hand for Mark
to sign.

When she had gone, Jacinth was busy with a column
of figures and an adding machine. Mark waited until she
had finished keying in numbers before he said quietly,
"Jacinth?"

"Yes?" She glanced up, her eyes remote, unrevealing.

"Does it matter whether I like you or not?"

She gave him a slightly derisive smile. "No. Of course
not. I was just—curious, that's all."

She turned back to her figures, and heard him say, almost under his breath, "Well, it's mutual, then."

CHAPTER SIX

THE wedding was an afternoon service attended by about fifty people, mostly friends of Lyle's. Jacinth, in turquoise lace, preceded her mother into the small church and found her eyes held by Mark's hard blue gaze as she walked steadily down the carpeted aisle. In a dark suit, and with a red carnation in his buttonhole, he looked particularly handsome and vital, and as she reached the chancel step and stopped, he gave her a strangely intimate little smile.

During the service, she tried to concentrate on her mother and Lyle, but Mark's tall presence intruded itself on her consciousness. After they had signed the register, he formally gave her his arm, as they followed the newly wedded pair back to the church door and paused there while photographs were taken. Several friends as well as the official photographer were busily snapping the wedding party.

"Smile," Mark said quietly, as someone called gaily, "Say cheese!" He added, "Try to look as though you're enjoying yourself."

"Are *you*?" she murmured, after she had obliged the photographers as best she could.

He glanced down at her, his eyes gleaming. "Of course. My father's wedding day, a beautiful girl on my arm . . ."

"Darrel said you don't notice pretty girls."

Lyle and Nadine were going down the steps, and Mark moved his arm to slip it about her waist. "Darrel talks a load of rubbish sometimes," he said. "I believe it's the

best man's privilege to claim a kiss from the bridesmaid."

She glanced up in alarm, involuntarily going rigid
against his encircling arm. Other men had looked at her
like that, with frank sexual curiosity, inviting her reaction. But not Mark. A wholly unfamiliar, shivery feeling
started in her stomach.

Mark laughed. "Never mind," he said. "It's way too
public here, anyway, for what I have in mind."

He drove her to the reception in his car. It was only a
short distance, and to her relief he concentrated on his
driving and didn't speak. By the time they got there she
had persuaded herself that she'd been imagining that
look. He had just been making the expected light small
talk outside the church.

A formal meal with a toast to the bride and groom and
a few speeches was to be followed by dancing. Mercifully
the speeches were short. Afterwards a cake was duly cut
by the bride and groom, and Jacinth organised a small
retinue of children to help her distribute the pieces. The
children, five of them ranging in age from about three to
ten, were obviously fond of Lyle and called him
"Uncle," but he told Jacinth he was actually their great-
uncle. "My sister's grandchildren," he explained.

"I really didn't think we should invite children at all,"
Nadine said to Jacinth under her breath. "But Lyle's
paying, after all, and I must admit, they seem well-
behaved."

"They're fine," Jacinth said. She liked children—she
could be natural with them, not feeling that she needed
to be on her guard. When the cake was all handed round,
the littlest one scrambled onto her knee and insisted on
giving her a sticky kiss. Laughing, she surreptitiously
wiped her cheek as he trotted away back to his mother,
then looked up to find Mark directing an odd, thoughtful look at her.

When Lyle and Nadine led off the first dance, Mark turned to Jacinth and said, "We're next, I believe."

For some reason she was reluctant to be held in his arms. She hesitated, and he said, "You can dance, can't you?"

"Yes." It was one of the skills her mother had insisted she should learn, sending her to ballroom dancing classes when she was twelve years old, even though the money for lessons was hard to find. Earlier, Nadine had managed somehow to pay for ballet lessons, but by the time Jacinth was ten it was already obvious that she was going to be tall, and Nadine reluctantly allowed her to give it up.

Mark put a hand on her waist and steered her towards the dance floor. Automatically she placed her right hand in his and her left correctly on his shoulder, and swung into the steps of the waltz. Most of the men she knew hadn't the faintest idea what to do with their feet unless they were dancing to a rock beat; slow numbers were merely an excuse to hold their partner in a more or less intimate embrace while shuffling about the floor. It was something of a treat to be partnered by a man who had mastered the art of more formal dancing.

"You're good," he said after a while, with scarcely hidden surprise.

He was, too, but she didn't say so, merely inclining her head in an ironic little acknowledgement of the compliment. He pulled her momentarily closer as a less skilled couple lurched dangerously alongside, and when the music stopped he said, "Don't go away. I'm enjoying this, aren't you?"

Without answering, she went into the curve of his arm again when the band began another tune. But at the next break, Darrel cut in, saying, "My turn, brother, you can't have the prettiest girl in the room to yourself all night."

Mark handed her over with a good grace, and she saw him presently take the floor with someone else. He danced with several women, one or two of them young and pretty, but others middle-aged, and he seemed intent, she thought, on charming them all. She didn't remember him ever directing that easy, relaxed smile at *her*.

She didn't lack for partners herself. Darrel wasn't quite as good a dancer as his brother, and he preferred to adopt a modern, hands-off style much of the time, but she didn't mind that. She accepted several other partners before Darrel claimed her again. Later he insisted on a third dance with her, this time a slow number, and he put both arms about her. She saw Mark standing on the sidelines for once, his narrowed gaze following them for a few minutes before the twirling couples hid him from her. When Darrel guided her off the floor, he kissed her cheek as he thanked her for the dance, then said, "You don't mind, do you? We're all family now, you know."

She smiled at him. "Of course I don't mind." It had surprised her a bit, but she wasn't offended. She could get fond of Darrel, perhaps of Lyle, too, who had been nice to her without false effusiveness, but Mark—Mark was a different proposition altogether.

Nadine and Lyle stayed until midnight, when the last dance was announced, and Jacinth found Mark at her side, his hand compelling her onto the floor.

"Tired?" he asked her.

"Not specially. Do I look it?"

His eyes inspected her rather thoroughly. "You look perfect—as usual. How do you manage it?"

Jacinth might have told him about the "beauty secrets" her mother had passed on, insisting that every woman should make the most of her looks, that there was no excuse for smudged lipstick or a shiny nose, although one should never make adjustments to one's appearance in public. Jacinth had been trained young—a hundred strokes of a hairbrush every night, well-cleaned teeth, all her clothes freshly ironed before she put them on and properly hung up as soon as she took them off, or promptly washed if there was a speck or a stain on them. And later, strict attention to grooming and carefully applied make-up. If she had ever questioned the need for women to be always smooth-skinned, sweet-smelling and attractive to men, by the time such thoughts surfaced the cultivation of feminine elegance had become second nature with her, and any sliding from the standards she had been set made her acutely uncomfortable.

Instead of telling him any of that, she said, "You sound as though you don't approve."

"I find it a little intimidating."

Intimidating! She laughed suddenly. She was quite sure Mark Harding never allowed anyone to intimidate him.

"That's a first," he said.

"What?"

"You've never laughed for me before. I like it."

She glanced up at him in slight confusion, then lowered her eyes again.

"What's the matter?" he said softly.

"Nothing." Something in his eyes disturbed her—a new, intent look that she hadn't seen before, even more disconcerting than the way he had looked outside the church. Surely Mark wasn't flirting with her?

"That colour suits you," he told her. "Makes your eyes look exactly the same shade. I always thought they were green—cat's eyes."

"My mother chose it," she said. Her eyes varied with her mood, from pure green to almost blue. She thought of them as an indeterminate sort of colour, neither one thing nor the other.

"It's the colour of the stone you're named for, isn't it?"

That surprised her. "Most people think of jacinth as orange or red."

"But it's thought to be the ancient name for blue zircon," he said. Her head lifted, and he held her gaze, a smile in his eyes. "I looked it up. There was a picture of the stone—green-blue, glossy and beautiful. Like a cool sea."

He swung her into a turn, and then his hand, which had been holding hers in a correct clasp, dropped to her waist, pulling her closer. Instinctively she put her palms against his shoulders, arching away slightly.

Mark smiled. "What are you stiffening up for?"

"I don't like dancing like this."

He took her hand again, but folded it against his jacket, and didn't increase the distance between them, his other arm firmly holding her to him. "Better?"

Stubbornly, Jacinth shook her head. "Not much."

He laughed softly. "You danced with Darrel like this."

"Darrel's different," she said involuntarily. Darrel hadn't made her feel breathless and trapped.

"Is that so?" Mark drawled. "In what way?"

Jacinth shrugged. "For one thing, he's much younger than you."

"Yes, that's right," he said, sounding thoughtful. "I'm very fond of my little brother, Jacinth. So take care."

Her head tipped back to look at him. "What do you mean by that?"

"I mean, don't hurt him."

"Why on earth would I want to hurt Darrel?" Genuine astonishment coloured her voice.

"Stop playing the innocent, Jacinth. You must be aware that Darrel is considerably smitten with you. And I've seen another poor sod in that condition, remember, getting the brush-off from you in no uncertain terms. Not a pretty sight."

Jacinth paled. "You had no right to listen in."

"I could hardly help it."

"You could have moved away."

"Rather obvious, don't you think? Anyway, I found it far too fascinating—if distinctly chilling."

She gave him a look that ought to have withered him on the spot.

Mark remained impervious. "Just remember," he said softly, "if you ever do that to Darrel, you'll have me to answer to."

Jacinth gave a scornful little laugh. Inwardly she was seething, but she was damned if she was going to let him guess how much he was getting under her skin. "He may be your little brother," she said, "but Darrel's over twenty-one, and I somehow don't think he'd thank you to fight his battles for him."

"I know his age," Mark answered sarcastically. "But he's been so busy studying since he left school—and before—that I don't think he's given himself much time to learn a lot about the opposite sex. In that area he tends to be rather naïve."

"Don't you think it's time you let him grow up?" With such a wide age gap between them, she supposed Mark must have developed the habit of protecting his brother, but surely this was excessive. And what on earth did he think she was, some kind of femme fatale? If she hadn't been so furious, it would have been funny.

Before the music stopped, Nadine and Lyle slipped away. A few people followed, but the happy couple were gone before a crowd could gather on the pavement. Lyle had everything well organised. Jacinth didn't know where they intended to stay tonight, but Nadine had told her in strict confidence that tomorrow they would be flying to Australia. Darrel was going to stay in the house until they returned, and then planned to move into a flat with friends.

"The departure seems to have gone without a hitch,"
Mark said, as the band packed up their instruments and
the guests gradually departed. "I'll just thank the band
and give them their cheque. Then I'll take you home."

"You don't need to," she said. "I'm sure someone
going that way can give me a lift."

"Best man's privilege," he said. "Stay put until I get
back."

She slipped into the Ladies' and lingered, hoping he
would think she had gone. She could always call a taxi.
Automatically she checked her appearance, renewed her
lipstick and smoothed her hair. Nadine had wanted her
to wear it loose, but eventually accepted a compromise,
in consultation with the hairdresser, who had pinned it in
a high Grecian knot entwined with turquoise ribbon and
allowed a loosely curled ponytail to swing against her
nape.

The band was clattering down the stairs with their gear,
and after that all became quiet. Jacinth waited a few
more minutes before emerging, hoping she hadn't left it
too long and got herself locked in.

"All set?" Mark asked, coming away from the wall he
had been leaning against, and unfolding his arms.

Jacinth nodded. There was no point in making it obvious, if he didn't already know it, that she had been
trying to avoid having him take her home.

The car purred up the slope to the house and swung
into the drive. "Nice," Mark commented appreciatively, nodding at the view. The air was especially clear
tonight, and cool. The lights of the city sparkled brightly,
and moonlight shone on the water of the harbour. "I'll
see you in."

She didn't object. He would do it anyway, she knew.
She had her key ready before he joined her on the small
veranda, but fumbled a little with the lock, because it was

dark. Mark stood by patiently, until she had reached in
and switched on the light by the door.

"Want me to come in?" he asked.

"What for?"

He grinned. "You're not nervous of being on your
own?"

"No, of course not."

"Of course not," he echoed, mocking her. Then he
said, "I wouldn't mind a coffee."

The light fell on his face, full of subtle male challenge. She knew that he expected her to refuse, and that
perhaps it would prove something to him. Perversely, she
said with an air of calm indifference, "All right. Come
on in."

He closed the door behind them, and followed her into
the kitchen.

She was filling the electric jug at the sink when she felt
a tug at the ribbon that held her hair, and jerked her head
aside, spilling some water. "What are you doing?" she
demanded. "Stop it!"

"I've had an overwhelming urge to do this all night,"
Mark said. Another tug, and the ribbon came free in his
hand. There were pins, too, of course, but without the
ribbon the knot loosened, and she felt the soft slide of
hair against her nape, her ears and cheeks. The ribbon
dangled in Mark's left hand, and his right hand deftly
removed a couple of pins.

She turned off the tap quickly and banged the jug
down on the counter. "Don't!" she said sharply, whirling to face him.

He was very close, laughing silently down at her, his
hand still in her hair. He raked his fingers through it, and
the remaining pins fell to the floor at their feet, one
pinging into the sink behind her.

"Sorry," he said, although obviously unrepentant. "I couldn't resist any longer. I used to pull the girls' pigtails at school."

"I don't doubt it," she snapped.

"Actually, that's a lie. I've often wondered what you'd look like with your hair down."

"Well, now you've satisfied your curiosity—"

He put his hands on the counter, trapping her within the circle of his arms. "And your lipstick smudged," he added softly, looking at her mouth.

Jacinth froze. Her heart seemed to lurch within her, and then settle to a steady pounding. She fought down a sudden, inexplicable panic. Mark wasn't a rapist. There was no need to scream and run, and yet she felt that if she moved, that was what she would do, fly at him like someone demented, make an utter fool of herself just because he had decided to indulge in a little masculine teasing. He was going to kiss her—so what? She had been kissed before. It was no big deal, nothing to make a fuss about, and when he found that he could elicit no response, he would leave her alone.

Slowly he raised his eyes until they met hers. His gaze narrowed, a faint line appearing between his brows. Abruptly, he moved away from her, the turquoise ribbon still dangling from his fingers.

Jacinth swallowed and turned to plug in the jug with shaking fingers. Distantly, she said, "Would you like a biscuit?"

It was a moment before he answered. "No, thanks, just coffee will do."

He was watching her, winding and unwinding her hair ribbon in his fingers. When she put the steaming cups onto a tray, he shoved the ribbon carelessly into his pocket and picked up the tray to carry it through into the other room.

It was quite cool in there, and she shivered and switched on the heater. Mark handed her cup to her, and they sat opposite each other, at first in silence. Eventually she said, ''It went off all right, the wedding.''

''Yes, without a hitch.''

There had been quite a lot of planning. Jacinth had been reluctantly involved to the hilt. She was glad it was over, but the wedding was only the beginning. There was still a tight little knot of anxiety inside her about her mother's future—and Lyle's.

As though he sensed it, Mark said, ''Relax, Jacinth. You're as taut as a violin string.''

She threw him a glance, but refrained from saying, Well, you're not helping. He had confused her today. Before, he had quite simply disliked her. It had seemed illogical, but she could cope with it. Now, in spite of his dislike, she was aware that somehow she had unwittingly intrigued him, aroused his hunting instincts. And that brought all her defences to the fore.

Perhaps he knew what was in her mind, though, because he put down his cup then and stood. ''I'll let you go to bed,'' he said. ''Thanks for the coffee.''

She said formally, ''Thank you for bringing me home.''

''Part of the best man's duties,'' he said lightly, moving to the door.

Automatically, Jacinth followed him into the hall. He opened the front door, and as she stood ready to close it behind him, he turned and raised his hand to smooth a wayward blond tendril from her cheek, tucking it behind her ear. ''Actually, it suits you,'' he murmured.

Jacinth willed herself to stay calm and unmoving. For a moment they faced each other like that, his fingers just touching the smooth skin below her ear. Then they slid to her chin, gently lifting it. Strangely, she thought the expression in his eyes was one of irritation. She made no attempt to evade his descending mouth, and when it touched hers it was warm and firm and searching—but the contact was very brief. ''The last of my duties—and privileges,'' he said dryly as he released her. ''Goodnight, Jacinth.''

When he had gone she leaned back against the door, thankful for something to support her. Dazedly, she thought, Mark? Mark Harding?

It wasn't possible. She must have been affected by the champagne that Lyle had provided for the celebrations. But drink had never had that effect on her before. Incredibly, shatteringly, when Mark Harding had pressed that fleeting kiss on her mouth, she had for a heart-stopping moment felt an urgent desire to kiss him back, to put her arms around him and hold his lips to hers.

She shook her head, and her hair swung against her nape, against her cheek, in unaccustomed, strangely sensuous freedom. A shiver ran down her spine, a combination of fear and excitement and sheer surprise holding her in its grip.

''Pull yourself together,'' she muttered aloud, and went into the other room to collect the cups, taking them to the kitchen. Her movements were slow and uncertain. Tiredness, she told herself, and reaction from the strain of the past few weeks when she had helped her mother prepare for the wedding.

Before getting into bed, she pulled back the curtains as usual, hating to wake to a darkened room. The streetlights and a few houselights still glowed and twinkled in the town. She stood watching them for a while, then sighed and turned away.

Across the river, in his modern flat, Mark Harding had discarded his jacket and tie, and was sitting on his bed frowning deeply, and absently smoothing a scrap of turquoise ribbon in his fingers.

CHAPTER SEVEN

ON MONDAY Jacinth thought that Mark looked at her rather searchingly when she arrived in the office, but otherwise he seemed just the same as before. Her own manner was cool and crisp, and she only spoke to Mark when necessary, on purely business matters.

Late in the afternoon, she had to ask him about a document that she needed.

"It's here on my desk," he said, looking up from what he was doing. Jacinth went over, saw it on top of a pile of papers, and reached for it just as he did the same. Their hands touched, and she snatched hers away as though she'd been burnt, instinctively straightening.

He picked up the paper and leaned back in his chair, staring at her. Jacinth put out her hand for the document. For a moment she thought he was going to keep holding it, but then he passed it over the desk. She knew he was still watching her as she walked away.

At the end of the day, he said, "Are you busy tomorrow night, Jacinth?"

"Why?"

"Cautious soul, aren't you?" he gibed. "Darrel and I thought you might like to have dinner with us, at Dad's place."

"Darrel—*and* you? Why?" she asked again.

The ghost of a smile touched his lips. "You could be missing your mother, and we might get to know one another a bit better."

"I thought you didn't like the idea of my getting to know Darrel too well," she said, a trifle waspishly.

His smile grew. "But I'll be there to keep an eye on you both."

"A chaperon?"

He laughed then. "I don't exactly see myself in that role."

She didn't, either. She didn't even know why she accepted the invitation. She refused his offer of transport, but the next evening she found herself driving to Lyle's house—her mother's house too, now. Already Nadine had placed a few of her own ornaments in the big lounge, and a scenic print she had always been fond of hung on the wall.

Mark noticed her looking at it. "Does it make you feel at home?" he asked, handing her a glass of wine as they waited for Darrel to put the finishing touches on the dinner.

She shrugged. "Actually, I never really cared for it very much."

He looked at the picture, then at her. "Mmm," he said thoughtfully, "I rather felt that your house was a setting for your mother, but not for you."

"It's my mother's house," she said, sipping at the wine he had given her.

Her mother's taste was excellent, but it ran to polished mahogany, patterned rugs and velvet upholstery, and antique furniture, which she coveted but had never been able to afford. Jacinth, while appreciating the beauty and craftsmanship of antiques, would have preferred to live with the clean, spare outlines and light colours of more up-to-date furnishings.

"You're going to stay on living there, aren't you?" Mark said. "You'll be able to redecorate if you want to."

"I don't know if I'll stay. I may look for something smaller, and newer."

"Have you always lived at home?"

"Except for the time I spent at university."

"What's your bedroom like?"

"What?"

"Your bedroom," he repeated patiently. "Weren't you allowed to do that up as you liked?"

"It's nothing special." Her mother had redone her bedroom while she was at university, as a birthday surprise in her second year. The old wallpaper with a pattern of ballet dancers in pink tutus had been replaced by a satin-finished, blue floral one, and her mother had made a frilled satin bedspread and new lace curtains. It was a pretty room for a teenage girl discovering her femininity, and it had been quite impossible for Jacinth to tell Nadine that she would have liked plain walls and cotton curtains, and a bedspread she could sprawl on with a cup of coffee and a bag of crisps and a book, one that would go in the washing machine and never crush or stain.

"You've lived away from here a fair bit, haven't you?" she asked him, to turn the conversation from herself.

"Off and on. I always seem to come back to the north, though," Mark said. "There's something about it. The warm climate, lazy summers, beaches, the occasional banana palm growing in a sunny corner, even if most of them never fruit. Here, I know I'm living in the Pacific. It's the nearest thing to being in the islands, I guess. And my mother's family has been here for generations. Her great-great-grandfather was a missionary at Kerikeri. We have numerous cousins in the area—you will have noticed at the wedding. I guess my roots are here, although I've done a fair bit of wandering."

"*My* mother's family are third generation," she said. "But most of them moved away. Like my father," she added with a touch of cynicism, and then wished she hadn't let her tongue run away with her, because Mark took her up on it.

"How old were you when he left?" he asked.

"Only four."

"Tough on your mother and you," he remarked.

"Yes. It was worse for her, of course. I don't remember much about it." She finished her drink, and he offered her another.

While she hesitated, Darrel came in and announced, "Dinner's ready. You can carve the pork, Mark, seeing the roast was your contribution. Besides, you're better at it than I am."

She had to compliment them on the meal. Roast pork and kumara with peas and potatoes wasn't ambitious, and they confessed that there was nothing home-made about the peaches and ice cream that followed, but between them they had produced a delicious dinner. Darrel said, "Mum insisted on us learning to cook, although Dad never rose to more than tinned soup and fried eggs. After she died, I took over the cooking until I left home for university, and then he got Mrs. McNab to help out."

"I expected to see her doing it tonight," Jacinth confessed.

Darrel gave her a theatrical leer. "Oh, no, my sweet bird! This way we have you all to ourselves, completely in our evil power."

"Cut it out, idiot," Mark said good-humouredly. "Jacinth was nervous enough of coming, without you confirming her dark suspicions."

"Nervous? Of us?" Darrel grinned at her. "You're not, are you?"

"Not of *you*," she said. "And of course I don't have any dark suspicions."

But Darrel was looking questioningly at his brother, even as she realised what she had just said. "What have you been doing to her, Mark?"

"Nothing," Jacinth answered for him hastily. "Mark's talking nonsense. He's just teasing."

She helped them to clear away the plates, which went into a dishwasher, and then they made coffee and took it into the other room.

Mark was being particularly nice to her tonight, talking as though they were real friends, leaning over to take her cup when she had finished her coffee, offering to get her another. Something in the very warmth of his manner bothered her, something that didn't quite ring true. It seemed to imply a closeness between them that didn't really exist, the implication becoming more obvious when once or twice he made some casual remarks about people or events at Pacific Trade Enterprises, and then turned to explain to Darrel what they were talking about.

When Jacinth rose to leave, Darrel said, "I'll walk you to your car."

"No need, little brother," Mark said. "I'm going, too. I'll see Jacinth safely off, first."

Darrel came to the door with them. "Good night, Jacinth," he said. "I hope we'll be seeing you often when the parents come back."

"Thank you again for the dinner. And a very pleasant evening."

"Any time." He bent and kissed her cheek.

"Come on." Mark's hand was on her waist. "Goodnight, Darrel."

Her car was behind Mark's in the driveway. Darrel was still standing on the lighted porch as she slipped the key in the lock of her car door. Mark leaned over and opened the door for her, his hair momentarily brushing her cheek as he bent past her. She flinched away from him, and when she made to get into the car, he barred her way with his arm as he rested a hand on the door.

He said, "You'll have to stop doing that, you know."

"What?" she asked, trying to sound totally uncomprehending.

"Jumping every time I touch you. And it is just me, isn't it? You don't do it with Darrel."

"I *like* Darrel."

There was a moment's silence. Then, his voice very clipped, he said, "Thanks."

Jacinth bit her lip. "I'm sorry."

He shrugged and stepped back. "I'll live. Drive carefully."

"Goodnight."

She got in, and he closed the door gently. She didn't look at him as she started the engine. He had asked for that, she told herself. And he wasn't hurt. He couldn't have been. Because he didn't care for her one bit, either; she was well aware of that.

She had put the car away and was walking to her own front door when she heard the cat. Something about the quality of the faint miaow made her stop, looking about in the darkness for its source. She and her mother had never owned a cat. Nadine didn't care for them in the house, and although like most children Jacinth had gone through a stage of wanting a cat or a dog, her mother had irrevocably vetoed the idea. Jacinth had to be content with dolls and the occasional opportunity to fondle her friends' pets.

The sound came again, with a definite quality of distress, and she said tentatively, "Puss? Puss, puss?"

Nothing. She took a few steps down the path, peering into the darkness, called again but received no answer. She waited a few minutes, went up the steps of the veranda and opened the door. Switching on the light, she hesitated, turned, thought a shadow moved near the gate. "Puss, puss, puss," she called, and the shadow came into the light. A small black cat, dragging one of its hind legs.

She started forward, and the cat stopped short and backed, crouching, as though it was about to flee.

Jacinth halted at the steps. "It's all right," she soothed. "I won't hurt you. Come on, puss, puss. Kitty, kitty, kitty." She backed up the steps again, and the cat stayed still, before moving cautiously closer. It stopped, sat and turned to lick at its leg, giving another of those pathetic miaows.

"What is it?" Jacinth said. "Did you have an accident? I wish you'd let me see. I might be able to help."

The cat looked at her, its eyes gleaming, and mewed, a more muted sound than its earlier cries.

For twenty minutes she coaxed it, even going into the kitchen to get a saucer of milk and place it at the bottom of the steps. Gradually it came closer, step by step, and at last condescended to drink some of the milk. One ear was bleeding, on the same side as the injured leg, and Jacinth guessed that it had collected a glancing blow from a passing car. Each time she moved from the top of the steps it skittered away, remarkably fast considering it was injured, and eventually she had to give up. Once she almost got a hand on it, but it hunched its shoulders, its fur rising aggressively, opened its pink mouth and hissed at her, so that she paused and it scuttled farther away. "Well, all right." She sighed. "But you're really a very stupid animal, you know. If you didn't want my help, why did you call me?"

She got up to go inside. The night was growing chilly, and she had gooseflesh on her arms. She turned to take a look at the cat again, wondering if she should find the SPCA number and phone them, but it was the middle of the night, and although its leg was obviously sore, it didn't seem desperately in pain. Perhaps if it was still hanging about in the morning... It probably had an owner around somewhere. By morning it might have recovered sufficiently to find its way home.

She turned to go in, and a black shape suddenly shot by, brushing her ankles, and into the hall.

It sat down at the other end and looked at her, its eyes green and glinting, daring her to do anything about it. It was a thin, unprepossessing animal, with bony shoulders and a long, white-smudged nose.

"Well!" Jacinth said sternly. "What happened to your limp? Five minutes ago I'd have sworn you'd never make it up those steps."

Its mouth opened in a loud, offended miaow; then it took two steps forward, awkwardly on three legs, and sat down again, its head drooping despondently to its breast. She moved towards it, and it cowered, shuffling backward with its leg at an angle, its eyes nervously wide.

"All right." Jacinth shut the door. "But if you scratch the furniture or make a mess, you're out on your ear, understand?"

The cat turned its head, presenting its torn and bloodied ear to her guilty gaze.

"Yes, that's all very well, but you won't let me near you to fix it, will you?" Jacinth said reasonably. "I just hope you don't get blood poisoning or something. And I've got to walk past you to get to my bedroom, so don't imagine you're going to be attacked, OK?"

It stood up and cowered against the wall as she passed, back arched, tail high, and its eyes suspicious, but when she came out of the bathroom it was sitting in the middle of the hall washing itself.

It stopped to watch her, and at the bedroom door she turned. "Goodnight," she said. "You con artist."

At ten minutes to six in the morning, she was woken by desperate yowls. Throwing back the blankets, she hurried anxiously into the hall to find the cat sitting at the front door, demanding to be let out.

"You horrible animal," she muttered, and opened the door. Stumbling back to bed, she thought she could have taken the chance to try to catch it, but at that hour she wasn't up to it.

Of course it was no good trying to go back to sleep, and by six-thirty she gave in and got up, showered and dressed. The morning paper would have arrived, and she could read it now instead of glancing at the headlines and waiting as usual until she got home tonight to read it properly. She opened the front door to find a pair of accusing green eyes regarding her from the bottom of the steps, where the cat sat in front of the empty saucer she had left there last night.

"Don't you have a home to go to?" she asked. Then, halfheartedly, "Go on—shoo!"

The cat blinked reproachfully, folded its tail more firmly about its haunches, and waited. Jacinth went to get the paper, pausing on the way back to say, "You know, if you have an owner waiting for you, I shouldn't feed you."

Its bony shoulders hunched pathetically, and a ripple ran over its skin, revealing every rib. She put out a hand to touch it, and it slithered away a few yards and stood with its injured leg lifted just off the ground, twitching its tail and looking half-starved and as though it expected to be beaten or kicked at any moment.

"You are impossible," Jacinth said, and went inside for some more milk. When she cautiously approached the little cat as it was lapping that, it warned her off with a low growl.

While Mark was at lunch, she telephoned the SPCA. The person who answered suggested that she make further efforts to capture the cat, and bring it in to them. If she had no success they would come out and attempt it themselves. But they seemed doubtful of finding it a home, if it was unclaimed by its owners. "Most people want a fluffy kitten. We'll probably have to put it down."

Jacinth hung up with some disquiet, hoping that the cat would be gone when she got home.

But it wasn't. It sat at the bottom of her front step, its eyes accusing her of culpable desertion and worse. "Hello," she said, attempting to stroke it. But it slunk away, and she saw that it was still limping, although the ear looked rather better. "You idiot animal," she said crossly. "Why can't you be sensible?"

It gave a sullen miaow, tucked its tail around its haunches, and fixed a baleful stare on her face. She tried to lure it into a cardboard carton with a tin of sardines, but although it went in, as soon as she began to fasten the flaps she had a battle on her hands. Howling indignantly, the cat scrambled and wriggled free, scratching her hand in the process, and shot off on three legs down the path to the gate, where it sat alternately washing itself vigorously and stopping to give her an unmistakably wrathful glare.

"I tell you, I won't hurt you!" she said, and it turned its head aside in patent disbelief, making her remember uncomfortably what the person at the SPCA had said about its likely fate. She picked up the half-finished tin of sardines and put it on the porch, away from the box. "Come on, then. Come and finish your dinner, anyway."

The cat ignored her, except for a twitch of its skinny tail and a distrustful blink of its eyes. In the end she gave up, left the tin and the milk, and shut the door firmly behind her.

On Thursday she stayed at her desk at lunchtime, looking through the yellow pages, and found a veterinarian whose surgery was not far from her home.

"Do you have a sleeping pill or something I could put in its food?" she asked. "Then if I brought it in you might be able to look at the leg."

"I can give you something that should slow it down a bit, if you call in after work," he said helpfully. "And you can borrow a cat cage, if you like."

"A cat cage sounds a wonderful idea," Jacinth said. "Thank you very much."

Mark had come into the room. "I didn't know you had a cat."

"I don't," she said, as she put down the phone. "It's a stray that's been hanging about, and I can't catch it."

He said, "Did it do that?" nodding at the long red weals on the back of her hand.

"Yes."

"I hope you disinfected it. Cat scratches can be nasty. Why do you want to catch it so badly? Is it being a nuisance?"

"It's hurt. All I want is to take the silly thing to the vet."

"And then?"

"I'll advertise for its owner. Although they'd be mad to claim it. I should think they're probably delighted that it's left."

Mark laughed, coming to half sit on her desk. "Not a nice, cuddly moggie, I take it."

"Cuddly! I'm sure it's trying to give me the evil eye. I think it was a warlock in another life."

He looked at her consideringly. "Not a witch?"

"It's male. I think."

"Have you looked?"

"I can't get close enough to look!"

"You got close enough to get scratched," he said, and he ran the back of his fingers lightly down the red marks on her hand. With an effort she stopped herself from snatching it away. Perhaps he noticed the sudden clenching of her jaw, because he took his hand away abruptly, and there was a tense little silence. Then he stood. "I'll come and help you catch it," he said, "if you like." And as she hesitated, he added, "I'm quite good with animals. They trust me."

Jacinth raised her eyes to his, and found a wry smile in them. He was mocking her, but not nastily. She found herself saying, "Thank you. I can probably use some help."

CHAPTER EIGHT

IT WASN'T easy, even with the help of the tranquilliser the vet had provided, and Jacinth had to make sure that the animal stayed in the house until the pill took effect, but at last, by a combination of cunning and force, the cat, obviously dopey but not asleep, was induced to enter the cage, and Jacinth triumphantly fastened the door on it.

"And it's no use looking at me like that," she told it, as it whirled round and gave her a look of pure venom. "It's for your own good."

Mark laughed. "I don't think she believes you."

"She?"

"I'll take a bet on it."

"No, thanks," she said. "My experience with animals is strictly limited. I expect you and Darrel were awash in dogs, cats and canaries when you were boys."

"Not exactly. But we certainly had pets. I was the only child for ten years, remember. My parents thought I needed animals, since I had no brothers or sisters, until Darrel came along."

"Did you mind?"

"What—being the only one? Did you?"

"I didn't mean that. I mean, did you mind when Darrel came along?"

"I don't remember minding. I was pretty tickled, actually. Although there hadn't been a lot of warning. My mother had suffered several miscarriages—something I didn't know then—so they didn't tell me until she was well on in the pregnancy that another member of the family was expected, and even then they played it down.

I guess they were afraid of something going wrong again. No, all I can recall is a sort of delighted surprise. He was quite a cute little beggar, young Darrel.''

She had wondered if there was some rivalry between the brothers; that would account for Mark's attitude to her when the three of them had spent the evening together. She was almost sure he had been doing it for Darrel's benefit, subtly linking himself with her, and putting Darrel on the outside. She remembered his warning to her at the wedding, and it suddenly occurred to her that he had been protecting his brother by implying a spurious interest in her himself. She cast him a coldly suspicious look, and he raised his brows and said, ''What's the matter?''

''Nothing.'' She looked away. ''Thanks for your help. I'll get this creature off to the vet.''

The cat had settled down, crouching on the bottom, sphinxlike, with its eyes half-closed.

''I'll come with you,'' Mark offered.

''I can manage now, thanks.''

''I'd like to come along, if it's OK. We can use my car, since it's parked behind yours.''

Reluctantly, she said, ''If you like.'' She didn't want to be actively rude to him, although she didn't quite understand why he was so keen to accompany her.

''What about you?'' he asked her when they were in the car, Mark having deposited the cage on the back seat.

He was reversing onto the road, and she waited for him to turn the car before she answered. ''What about me?''

''You didn't answer my question. Did you mind being an only child?''

''Not usually.''

''Your mother told us that you and she were always very close.''

''Yes.''

''You don't have many friends, do you?''

"Did she tell you that, too?"

He hesitated. "In a roundabout sort of way."

"Most of my friends live elsewhere now. I had friends at school. And university. I still write to a couple of them."

"What about since you moved back here?" he asked her. "I rather gathered that Nadine thought you might pine for her after she married my father. She seems to think that you're—dependent on her."

She wondered if she was imagining the ironic undertone in his voice that she frequently thought she heard when he spoke of Nadine. As the car slowed for the turn onto the main road she said, "Do I strike you as a dependent sort of person?"

He looked at her with a faint smile. "No," he said frankly. "I must admit the idea surprised me. I'd have thought it was more likely the other way around."

"Quite," said Jacinth, and he cast her a sideways glance and lapsed into silence.

Mark was right about the cat's sex, the vet confirmed. He looked at the ear, swabbed it with disinfectant, carefully examined the leg, and then the rest of the body, even taking its temperature while the animal flattened its ears and kept up a low, growling whine. "Nothing broken," he said. "She's underfed, and a bit dehydrated at the moment. But there's no sign of fever. The leg should come right. The muscles are pulled, and she's bruised. The injuries were probably caused by a car, or possibly she's been in a fight, but I'd say she hasn't been particularly well cared for, before that. She's spayed, though. Are you going to keep her?"

"I suppose you wouldn't know of a good home?" Jacinth asked, without much hope.

"'Fraid not. I'll put her down for you, if you like, no charge. Seems a pity, as she's basically a healthy young animal. But if you want to keep her, I'd advise a couple of vaccinations, in case she hasn't had them.''

"I—don't really want a cat," Jacinth said.

"OK." He shrugged, and picked it up off the stainless steel table. With instinctive compunction, Jacinth put out her hand to touch its black head as the vet turned towards the cage and opened the door. The cat's mouth opened, showing sharp little teeth, and it hissed at her, struggling in the vet's expert hold. As he shifted his grip to put it in the cage, it gave a peevish howl, and its claws opened, hooking into the edges of the cage, so that he had to pause and disengage them.

The little cat twisted in his hands, and climbed onto his shoulder, digging its claws into his white coat, and caught Jacinth's eyes with a wide, green stare.

"But I'll keep it until I can find someone who does," Jacinth said hastily as he hauled it down.

"The stuff's wearing off," the vet commented, wincing as a claw raked his wrist.

He lent Jacinth the cage again, and she promised to return it the following morning. She wrote a cheque for the treatment, and as they drove back to her place, she said to Mark, "I suppose *you* don't want a cat?"

"I'm away too much," he said. "What are you going to call it?"

"I'm not going to call it anything. I'm just going to look after the wretched animal until it recovers, and then I'll find it a home." She wouldn't be trying to find its original owner. If it hadn't been looked after, she wasn't going to send it back to a life of neglect.

A loud howl and a threatening rattle from the cage on the rear seat announced that its occupant was now well and truly awake. "Who with?" Mark asked, grinning. "A nice young family? A sweet little old lady?"

She looked at him coldly. Obviously this wasn't that kind of cat. One didn't wish a suspicious, ungrateful, bad-tempered, fiendishly cunning reincarnated witch onto the unsuspecting parents of young children, or innocent old ladies.

"I think she's chosen you," Mark said.

"Chosen?"

"Don't you know about cats?" he said. "They may choose to let someone feed and house them, but you don't own them. Even the law recognises that a cat can't be fenced in. A dog owner is legally responsible if his pooch trespasses on your property, but cats are exempt."

Another yowl from behind them made Jacinth turn around. "It's all right," she said. "We're nearly there. And you needn't look at me like that. You ought to be grateful that I decided to bring you home again. Not to mention spending a small fortune on you."

Mark cast her an odd look. "Why did you?" he asked quietly.

"Didn't you see how it looked at me?"

"Ah! Pleading?"

"Good Lord, no! It tried that the first night, but it knows I've cottoned on to that little game. No, more like 'I'll get you for this, you see if I don't!' I was afraid she'd haunt me."

Mark was laughing. "This promises to be an interesting relationship."

"This is not a relationship. It's a temporary association."

"As I said, you don't know cats."

After Mark had carefully opened the cage and watched the cat fly off into the shrubs near the gate, as quickly as its injured leg would allow, Jacinth asked him, "Would you like some tea—dinner?" It was the least she could do, after accepting his help. And it was getting late now.

"Thanks," he said. "If it's not too much trouble." He was gazing after the cat. "I suppose she'll come back when she's forgiven us."

"With any luck, she never will," Jacinth replied, and went inside to see what she could find in the kitchen.

They had fillet steak, and so did the cat, when she came to the door later, demanding to be fed.

Mark raised his brows at that. "Fillet?"

"I don't have cat food in the house," Jacinth said. "I don't *have* a cat, for heaven's sake."

"You do now," Mark pointed out. "What have you fed her on so far?"

"Tinned fish, mostly," she told him. "Sardines—and a few scraps."

He carried his plate to the sink, and saw the empty tin soaking there, labelled Fancy Pink Salmon. "Sardines?" he queried, holding it up.

She had opened it this morning, not being able to find anything else to give the cat.

"The condemned's last meal," she said. "At least, it was supposed to be. I had to give it *something*."

"What a surprising person you are, Jacinth," he said slowly.

"Am I?" Suddenly wary, she made her eyes blank. "You could probably say that of most people."

"Fascinating," he said. "Your eyes have gone just like Hecate's."

"Hecate?"

"An appropriate name for your cat, I thought. Hecate was the goddess of witches—and you do seem to credit your little cat with supernatural powers."

"It's not *my* cat!"

He chuckled. "Nobody else's, my pet."

Jacinth blinked. What an extraordinary thing to call her, she thought. "And *I'm* not your pet!"

"Sorry," Mark said ruefully. "It just slipped out."

"I suppose it's what you call your girlfriends," she said scornfully.

"You make it sound as though I have them by the score."

"Don't you?"

Mark's brows rose. "Why the sudden interest in my love life? Dare I hope you're jealous?"

"No, you daren't!" she snapped. "Although you're not above taking an interest in mine, are you?"

"Meaning the first time we met?"

"Yes."

"That was an expression of a general interest in human nature, I'm afraid." He paused. "Does it still rankle?"

"It—wasn't very nice," she said lamely.

"Strangely enough, I thought that about you," he said. "At the time."

"Does that mean you've changed your mind since?"

"Let's say, I'm reserving judgement."

She felt a flicker of anger. "What a prig you are, Mark," she scoffed. "By what conceivable right do you sit in judgement on me? Or anyone?"

A faint, dark colour came into his face. "I didn't mean it like that."

"That's the way it sounds."

"Then I'm sorry."

Jacinth shrugged indifferently. "It doesn't matter."

A faint smile curved his mouth. "In other words, you don't really give a damn what I think of you."

She met his eyes with a cool smile of her own. "No, actually. Do you mind?"

"What a very civilised quarrel this is," he remarked conversationally.

"Is it a quarrel?"

"Oh, I think so," he said. "Underneath that cucumber-cool of yours, you're hopping mad with me, aren't you? So why not let it all out?"

"Not my style," she said mockingly. "Besides, didn't we just agree that I don't care what you think of me? And if I don't care, why should I get mad?"

"Mmm. Why indeed?" he murmured. "Unless, perhaps, you're not quite so unfeeling as you like to pretend."

Deep inside her she felt a tremor of something like fear. "You're talking nonsense."

"Am I?" He looked sceptical. "To be honest, the first time I saw you, I thought, That girl is the most beautiful thing I've ever seen."

A flash of surprise lit her eyes, before she looked quickly away.

"Then," Mark said, "I watched you, and saw that poor guy pleading for a crumb of kindness from you—and not getting it. And I thought, beautiful—and ice-cold."

He had called her a "cold bitch", that day he came to the office. She had known then that it wasn't just because of her attitude about the Bayside Boats account. For some reason her apparent coldness had angered him.

"Life is full of disappointments," she said, keeping her voice light.

"That's why," Mark added deliberately, "when I saw Darrel falling at your feet, I was worried for him."

"You needn't be," she said. "I'm no danger to Darrel."

He pursed his lips and looked her over, slowly, from head to foot and back again. Then he said softly, "Jacinth—you're a danger to any man. And I can't believe that you're unaware of it."

He was telling her clearly that he found her attractive. But he neither liked nor trusted her. Whatever game he was playing, she sensed that it was at least equally dangerous for her.

"Leave the dishes," she said abruptly. "I'll do them in the morning. It was kind of you to come and help with the cat. Thank you."

He laughed down at her. "And goodnight? Getting too close to the bone, are we?"

"I have no idea what you're talking about."

She turned, pointedly waiting for him to leave, and he said, "OK, I'll take the hint."

He strolled past her to the front door, and Jacinth followed.

"See you tomorrow," he said, opening the door.

"Yes." She was standing well back, waiting to close the door after him.

He stopped with his hand on the latch, and looked at her. "I won't bite," he said.

She didn't move and didn't answer. The cat came up the steps, surprisingly agile for all its limping gait, then, as he turned to look at it, fled to the path again.

Mark glanced back at Jacinth. "You and Hecate have a lot in common," he said. "You should get on well together."

CHAPTER NINE

NADINE was horrified when she learned about Hecate. "A cat! Not even a decent Persian or a Siamese! A stray off the street? Oh, really, Jacinth, whatever possessed you?"

"An evil spirit, I shouldn't wonder," Jacinth murmured.

"What?" Nadine stared at her, uncomprehending.

"Nothing. She's house-trained, and anyway, most of the time she's outside."

"But all the same, darling! They scratch things, you know, and what about fleas?" They were standing in the kitchen, where Hecate had been washing herself on the mat outside the back door until Nadine appeared, when she promptly bolted into the gathering dusk. It was Nadine's first visit since she and Lyle had returned from their honeymoon.

"I haven't noticed any fleas, and—" Jacinth surreptitiously crossed her fingers "—she hasn't damaged any of the furniture." She had found scratch marks on one of the veranda posts yesterday, but she hoped her mother wouldn't see them. "Anyway, I'm not going to keep her. It's just until I find someone who wants a cat."

"It might be diseased—a stray."

"The vet checked her over. She's quite healthy. That's why I didn't like to let him put her down."

"Well, I hope you find a home for it soon. I thought I'd take the blue vase and the Wedgwood dishes. And the rest of my clothes, of course. Help me pack them, would you, darling?"

Later, as she was leaving, she turned to peck Jacinth's cheek. "Oh, we're having a family dinner on Saturday night. About seven. The boys and you. You're not doing anything, are you?"

The boys, Jacinth supposed, meant Darrel and Mark. She didn't know why she was reluctant to go, but it wasn't any use saying she was busy. Her mother would simply choose another date.

She said, "Shall I bring something?"

"No, of course not. I'm cooking you all a very special dinner."

If the way to a man's heart was through his stomach, Nadine had the route well mapped. Jacinth knew her mother was a wonderful cook, but on Saturday night she outdid herself. After serving them a creamy asparagus soup, followed by coq au vin and a rich, layered dessert full of fruit and cream, she glowed at the compliments the men showered on her. Sending them into the lounge, she let Jacinth help her serve cups of properly percolated coffee with cream, and a dish of mints.

Mark, taking a mint from the plate Jacinth offered him, said quietly, "I take it your mother disapproves of Hecate."

She had heard her mother say something about "an awful little half-wild cat" at dinner, but she had been talking to Darrel at the time.

"*I* don't approve of Hecate," she said. "I certainly don't expect my mother to take that unnatural creature to her bosom."

"Give them time. Hecate may yet creep into her heart."

"You know perfectly well," Jacinth retorted, "that nothing is less likely."

He looked thoughtfully across the room at Nadine, who was smiling at Darrel with a look less motherly than flirtatious. It was the way she looked at all men, young or old, as natural to her as breathing. Mark grinned suddenly. "No," he agreed. "Nadine would prefer something a good deal less aggressive than Hecate—a white Persian, perhaps."

"So would *I* prefer a white Persian, or a black Persian—anything more civilised than that devil's daughter that's been wished on me. So would anyone in their right mind."

"Still haven't coaxed her onto your knee, then?" he teased.

"I wouldn't even try! I value my skin—and my panty hose—more than that. I can't wait to find someone who will take her off my hands."

"You've been saying that for—what is it?—almost two weeks by now, surely?"

He had asked after the cat each day, and although she reported the leg was getting better and its coat was less dull, it still backed suspiciously from an outstretched hand, even while stalking in and out of the house as if it owned the place.

"I'm counting the days," she assured him, and moved on to offer the sweets to Darrel.

Darrel and Mark gathered up the coffee cups and took them to the kitchen, and Nadine showed Jacinth pictures of herself, which Lyle had taken against a variety of scenic backgrounds. Nadine had enjoyed a shopping spree in Sydney, and then they had hired a car and seen all the usual tourist spots in the area.

Lyle left the room for a few minutes as Nadine was opening the second packet of photographs. "It was a lovely holiday," she said with a sigh, "and Lyle is such a considerate man. Look, he gave me this." She lifted her arm to show off a gold and pearl bracelet.

"It's beautiful."

"Isn't it?" She turned her arm appreciatively. "He adores me."

"You do love him, don't you?" Jacinth asked.

Nadine looked at her with pained surprise. "But, darling, of course I do!" She dropped her arm and looked speculatively at her daughter. "How are you getting on with Mark?"

"With Mark? All right."

"Only all right? I know you have a rather unfortunate manner with men, but you work with him, and I'm married to his father. I must admit, I'd hoped that you and he might become good friends."

"We're perfectly friendly."

A tiny frown appeared between her mother's brows. She said chidingly, "Really, darling, I do think you could make more of an effort. A man needs a bit of encouragement. Looks alone aren't enough."

Patiently, Jacinth said, "I've no intention of 'encouraging' Mark, Mother. It isn't that sort of relationship."

Nadine sighed. "I suppose it's too much to expect you to put yourself out to attract a man."

"Yes," Jacinth said shortly. "Especially Mark."

"Why 'especially Mark,' for heaven's sake?" her mother almost wailed.

"For one thing, we work together. And I've already had some experience of what complications can arise from that. Don't worry about me. I'm quite happy as I am."

"You may be now, but wait until you're older, and lonely."

Something in her voice made Jacinth pause.

"Were you frightened of that?" Jacinth asked. "For yourself?"

"You don't know what it's like," Nadine said fretfully, "to be growing older and losing your looks—and not have anyone."

"No, I suppose not," Jacinth said slowly, groping towards an understanding of her mother.

"But if you're going to be too choosy, it could happen to you," Nadine warned. "Feminists can say what they like, men just don't like women to be too self-sufficient."

Jacinth refrained from saying that a good many feminists weren't particularly bothered by what men liked or didn't like. "I'm sure you're right," she murmured.

She was relieved when the men came back to the room, although when Mark quirked a smile at her, her answering smile was rather stiff. She couldn't help knowing that Nadine's eyes were on them, alert for any sign that her motherly strictures had fallen on receptive ears.

"Something wrong?" he said, disconcertingly choosing to sit beside her on the sofa.

Jacinth shook her head. "No, nothing."

He looked at her thoughtfully, then glanced at her mother, who was showing Darrel the photographs now, as Lyle perched on the arm of her chair. Softly, he said, "Are you still bothered about this marriage?"

"What makes you think I was ever bothered by it?"

Mark pursed his lips. "I just had a feeling, the night they announced their wedding plans, that you were more than slightly thrown."

"It was a bit sudden, that's all. I told you at the time, I was surprised. So were you."

"Yes," he said, after a brief pause. "But that wasn't what surprised me." He stood up suddenly, saying, "Come with me. There's something I want to show you."

He bent to take her hand, and pulled her to her feet. "We won't be long," he said to the others. "We're just going out to my car for a minute."

His fingers were strong and warm about hers. She made a small effort to draw away, but he didn't seem to notice. "Come on," he said.

In his car, he put her in the passenger seat, slid in beside her and leaned over to bring a large envelope from the glove box. "My father gave me these earlier tonight," he said. "He wants me to take care of them." He tipped out a number of folded papers and some photographs. Switching on the interior light, he selected one of the photographs, and handed it to her. "My mother."

Jacinth studied the picture. The woman in it must have been about thirty at the time it was taken. She had dark hair, pulled back rather severely from a strong-boned face. There was a strange, compelling attraction about the face, with its fine, dark brows and steady eyes that looked straight into the camera, and a firm mouth holding a hint of a smile. She could see a resemblance in her elder son, but that wasn't why he had shown it to her. This woman looked like Nadine's opposite.

She looked up and handed the photograph back. "Yes," she said. "I see why you were surprised."

"I thought you would."

"It doesn't mean your father can't be perfectly happy with a different kind of woman."

"It doesn't mean anything," he agreed. "I just thought it interesting."

"Yes."

She shifted restlessly, placing her hand on the door handle.

"Why are you nervous of me?" Mark asked.

"I'm not." Defiantly, she looked him in the eyes.

"You can't spend five minutes in my company without shying away. Even when I took your hand just now, I felt your fingers go tense."

Ostentatiously, she removed her hand from the door, folding it in her lap with the other. "I spend hours in your company for five days of every week."

"Yes, and whenever I come within two feet, I can feel the vibrations."

She hadn't thought that he knew. At work he treated her with a slightly impersonal friendliness, which she tried hard to match.

"Am I physically repulsive to you?" he asked her abruptly. "Tell me the truth."

Numbly, she shook her head. "Of course not."

Something gleamed in his eyes. "That's a relief. You had me worried for a while. Tell me about Philip, Jacinth."

"Tell you what?"

"What your relationship was, what happened between you."

"That's none of your business."

For a moment Mark rested his forehead on spread fingers. "OK, I suppose you're right," he admitted, looking up again. "Shall I tell you something? Ever since I heard Philip say, 'You were so passionate last night, in my arms,' I've wondered what it was like. You sat there like a statue carved in ice, as though you'd never had a passionate moment in your life, and yet he was shaking with the memory. What *is* it like, Jacinth?"

Jacinth felt her face go cold and pale. *It was a sham, I was pretending.* But she couldn't tell him that. She couldn't. She shook her head, her voice reduced to a whisper. "You'll never know."

His head went up slightly, his eyes narrowing. "Is that a challenge?"

She hadn't meant it to be. "I'm going in," she said in a stifled voice, fumbling open the door.

"Running away?"

She turned her head to look at him. "Terminating a pointless conversation," she said, and got out of the car, closing the door behind her.

He caught up to her before she reached the front door, which he had left on the latch. When she made to open the door, he said, *"Come here!"* and grabbed her wrist, whirling her round and into his arms. As her lips parted in astonished protest, he covered them with his, and this time he wasn't playing. It was a long, thorough and very expert kiss.

For the first couple of seconds she was too surprised to react at all. Then she instinctively stiffened, her hands pushing against him. He merely shifted his grip without taking his mouth from hers, one arm tucking her head immovably into the curve of his shoulder, the other hand taking possession of her wrists.

Her mind was seething with a mixture of anger and astonishment—anger because he had not asked for her consent; and astonishment because her fury was shot through with sharp, bright, spinning stars of pleasure and excitement.

In spite of that, in spite of the patient coaxing of his lips on hers, she refused him the satisfaction of a response, holding on to her pride and her anger, and when he slowly let her go, he looked at her searchingly, then smiled. "You can do better, I'm sure," he drawled. "You weren't really trying, Jacinth."

"You noticed! Well, if *you* were, you have a lot to learn!" she shot back.

He laughed aloud. "I promise I'll try to improve next time."

About to give the obvious retort, she bit it back. Mark would always rise to a challenge. It would be simply silly to issue such a predictable one. She pushed at the door, which swung open, and the light spilled out of the hall. "You have lipstick all over your mouth!" she whispered fiercely to him.

He lifted his fingers and wiped the pink smear away. "And you, darling," he said, with blatant enjoyment, "haven't."

She stopped in the doorway. Damn him! Her mother would be sure to notice, even if the others didn't. Her small bag was in the living room, by the chair she had taken when she first walked in. Well, she would just have to brazen it out. Her face a distantly aloof mask, she lifted her head and walked ahead of Mark into the room.

"And what have you two been up to?" Nadine said archly.

Jacinth glanced at Mark. He looked, she thought, sickeningly pleased with himself. Darrel glanced quickly from him to Jacinth and back again.

"Looking at some photographs," Mark said. "Seeing your holiday snaps reminded me I had a couple in the car that I thought would interest Jacinth."

"Oh?"

Obviously Nadine was about to ask more questions, but a swift look passed between Mark and his father, and when Mark said, "And I haven't looked at yours properly, yet—may I?" Lyle ably helped him to change the subject, and had soon drawn Nadine into a detailed description of their holiday.

CHAPTER TEN

MARK was going north to check progress on the schooner being built by Bayside Boats. "I'd like you to come," he told Jacinth.

"What for?" She turned in her chair, looking across to where he sat glancing through the mail Rosa had placed on his desk.

"You know better than anyone what their financial position is. You also know ours now. We need this schooner, Jacinth."

"I'm not their accountant any more. Things may have changed."

He looked at her. "I want you to come, OK?"

Jacinth shrugged. "You're the boss."

His eyes gleamed, his mouth compressing slightly, and she said, "When?"

"Thursday, I thought, if that suits you. It's only going to be a day trip. Don't come into the office that morning. I'll pick you up."

He arrived a little early, rang the bell at the front, and followed Jacinth through to the kitchen.

Hecate's dishes were now on the porch at the back door, and she sat on the lowest step, her tail twitching impatiently.

"Still here, I see," Mark commented, strolling to the door as Jacinth poured milk and spooned out cat food. Hecate raised her head to give him a basilisk stare and, apparently deciding he was neutralised, slipped up the steps and began to eat.

"How long is it now?" Mark asked. "Three weeks?"

"About." Jacinth shrugged, her eyes daring him to say, "I told you so."

He gave her a faint smile, and went down on his haunches to look more closely at the cat. "She's put on weight."

Hecate bristled and emitted a low snarl.

"All right," Mark said. "I'm not planning to take your breakfast away from you."

He straightened slowly to avoid startling her, and Jacinth said, "I'm just going to get my jacket and bag. Lock that door for me, would you?"

"Sure," he said over his shoulder, his eyes still on the cat.

She could hear his voice as she tidied the cover on the bed, checked the room and her own appearance, in a slim red skirt and cream blouse, and picked up a navy-blue jacket and her shoulder bag.

Returning to the kitchen, she was brought up short in the doorway. Hecate, her back ecstatically arched, tail at attention, was rubbing herself against Mark's trousered legs, as he stood with his hands in his pockets, murmuring quietly to her.

"How in the world did you do that?" she asked.

"I told you I was good with animals." He bent down and scratched with his fingers just behind the cat's ear. "She likes me, don't you, girl?"

Jacinth blinked. A strange sound was emanating from the cat. "Good heavens!" she exclaimed. "She's purring."

"So she is. We'd better be going, if you're ready." Gently, he steered Hecate towards the door with his foot. "Sorry, girl. We have to leave now."

She looked up at him, gave a little purring meow, and trotted obediently out of the door.

"I don't believe it!" Jacinth said. "She still backs off if I try to stroke her."

"Try letting her make the approach. She will. Talk to her a lot, and gain her confidence."

Jacinth was sceptical. "I *have* talked to her."

"Ah, but perhaps you don't use the right words. Females respond to sweet-talk, you know."

She cast him a withering look, saw that he had his tongue firmly in his cheek, and refused to rise to his teasing.

Ted and Oscar were pleased and surprised to see Jacinth again. They treated her and Mark to morning tea, served in thick china cups and accompanied by a pile of sticky buns and oozing cream cakes from a nearby take-away bakery. Mark inspected the half-finished hull, held in a huge cradle inside a hangarlike building, and tried to explain to Jacinth where the wheelhousing, the living accommodation and storage space would be, and the relationship between the various parts. In the cluttered little office afterwards, Ted produced a neatly clipped and labelled pile of invoices for them to check, and Mark wrote out a cheque for the next batch of necessary materials.

"We're doing everything like you said," Ted told Jacinth. "And the books are checked every month by your Mr. Rotch."

Jacinth saw the quick glance Mark slanted at her, but ignored it.

"We're not out of the woods yet," Oscar admitted, "but it looks like we might make it."

"I'm very glad," Jacinth told them.

"They like you," Mark commented, as he and Jacinth returned to his car, parked on the main street of the little town.

"You sound surprised," she said, rather tartly.

"Maybe I am."

"Not everybody shares *your* taste," Jacinth retorted, more hurt by such bluntness than she would ever have admitted.

He had let her into the car and slid in beside her before he answered. Then he turned in his seat, and said, "You misunderstood me. I meant that those two and you are so different—they're brilliant boat builders and good blokes, and the term 'rough diamond' might have been coined for them. Frankly, I'd expect them to be rather cowed by you."

"Cowed?" Oscar was six feet four in his boots, with hands the size of dinner plates, and wore extra-large shirts that strained at the buttons. His brother was not much smaller.

"There's nothing like a beautiful woman with class, brains and a head for figures to reduce someone like that to mumbling incoherence."

Such a run of compliments was about more than she could take, Jacinth thought. "I don't seem to have that effect on you."

"No," he agreed musingly. "The effect you have on me is quite different."

She turned on him a look of aloof enquiry.

"No," he said, his eyes very blue and holding a hint of laughter. "I don't think I will tell you—just now."

Consumed with curiosity, she nevertheless managed a convincingly indifferent shrug, turning away from him. Out on the harbour, a number of yachts, some with brightly coloured sails, rode at anchor on calm water, the ripples breaking their reflections into confettilike pieces. The scene was peaceful in the extreme, and she couldn't understand why she should feel a rising tide of some kind of excitement mixed with trepidation, as though a wild storm were about to break. She swallowed, trying to force it down.

"Lunch," Mark said. "A nice, leisurely one, I think."

Jacinth looked at her watch and saw with surprise that it was after one o'clock. "Shouldn't we be getting back?"

"We have to eat. And by the time we do that and drive back, the day's practically over. Why don't we take the afternoon off?"

"You're the boss."

"Original," he said dryly. "Can't you muster any more enthusiasm than that?"

"What do you want me to do? Fall on your neck with tears of gratitude?"

"Now, that might be interesting."

"Sorry. I'm not the tearful type."

"No, you're not, are you?"

"You sound regretful," Jacinth said, with light mockery. "Do you like women who cry all over you?"

"I don't recall that it's ever happened."

"You surprise me."

His brows rose; then suddenly he laughed. "Jacinth, you never cease to surprise *me*!" He started the car. "I believe there's a restaurant that's not too bad, over in the next bay."

Their lunch was a light one of chicken salad, accompanied by a half-carafe of good white wine. The restaurant was housed in an old building overlooking a tranquil harbour, where a few fishing boats and pleasure launches rocked on the gentle waves. Next door was a craft shop selling pottery and carved kauri bowls, and a little farther along the road were a few other shops serving a small local population and the passing tourist trade.

"Dessert?" Mark asked her.

Jacinth shook her head. "I don't go much for sweets."

His mouth quirked, and he seemed about to say something, and then to change his mind. They had coffee, and Jacinth went into the ladies' room. She noticed a run in her tights, and took them off, discarding them in a metal bin under the counter. She always carried a spare pair, but decided not to bother. Although summer was waning, this far north the weather was still balmy and warm, and outside the sun was shining. She had taken off her jacket at lunch, finding the restaurant quite hot.

When they emerged into the sunlight, though, the sea breeze had freshened, and she quickly slipped her jacket back on. Mark said, "What would you like to do? And don't tell me I'm the boss. As of an hour or so ago, we're officially off duty."

"All right," she said. "I'd like to buy a pair of shoes."

"Shoes," he repeated blankly, looking down at the high-heeled navy leather pumps she was wearing.

"And then walk," she added.

"Walk? Where to?"

"Wherever there is."

"Breaking out, are you?" He began to smile.

"Oh, riotously. I won't be long."

His brows rose. "Are you planning to take this hike on your own?"

"You know that isn't what I meant. You wouldn't want to watch me trying on shoes."

"Of course I would. Didn't know I was a secret foot fetishist, did you?"

She couldn't help laughing, and he said, "I wish you'd do that more often."

"There isn't often anything to laugh about."

"What a limited life you lead, Jacinth."

"What a decadent one *you* lead!"

He laughed outright at that, throwing back his head. "I assure you, far from it." Then, taking her arm, he said, "Come on, let's see about these shoes."

There wasn't much choice. Only two of the small huddle of shops stocked shoes. One was a boutique selling holiday clothes, tie-dyed cotton skirts, T-shirts and silk scarves, where she found only glamour sandals, and the other was a general store selling groceries, clothing and hardware, and with a muddled corner featuring mainly gumboots, sneakers and coloured slippers with pompoms on the front. After poking round the dusty boxes, Mark pulled one out and opened it, to display a pair of cream canvas espadrilles. "What about these?" he suggested.

Replacing a pair of sneakers she had found, she asked, "Do they have a size marked on the box?"

"Five," he answered, after a cursory look.

"Well—maybe."

She looked about, didn't see a chair and, standing on one leg, took off a shoe. She held out her hand for the box, but he said, "Let me," and knelt on the gritty floor, placing the box beside him to lift out one of the espadrilles.

His hand grasped the bare skin of her ankle firmly, and her mouth went suddenly dry. The shoe slipped on, and he released her foot and said, "Better try the other one."

Silently she let him put it on for her, staring down at the dark head bent to his task.

"There you are," he said, and stood up. "How do they feel?"

"Fine."

"Take a bit of a walk round in them."

She turned away from him and walked to the other end of the shop and back. She didn't look at him, but she knew he was watching her all the way.

"I'll take them," she said, and he picked up the box from the floor and dropped her discarded shoes into it.

"Your trousers are dusty," she pointed out to him, and he brushed at the soiled knees of his jean-style corduroys with his hand. Then he stood by holding the box while she paid for the espadrilles.

* * *

They strolled along the wall of the harbour first. Mark
had put her shoes in the car, and she had left her bag
there, too. A stone breakwater had been built, the water
lapping at a narrow strip of muddy sand just below it.
Pohutukawas grew along the road's edge, their branches
romantically framing glimpses of the harbour, and the
brittle, silver-backed leaves making tiny clacking noises
in the breeze that lifted off the water. A wide old wharf
of greasy, ridged timber stretched out into the water.
They stepped onto the weathered planks and walked to
the end of it, where a fishing boat was moored and plas-
tic containers of shiny silver fish were being handed up to
helpers on the wharf. Looking between the uneven grey
boards as they walked, Jacinth could see the water below, green and rippling. As the unloading was completed, they leaned over the rail on the side of the wharf,
watching a school of tiny bright fish flashing in and out
of the greening piles.

Sunlight glinted on the water. The smell of fish was
strong, and a launch travelling slowly towards a small,
humped island offshore set the water under the wharf
chuckling and swishing round the piles, and hissing up
onto the shallow slope of the shore. The tiny fish darted
away, disturbed, and Jacinth looked after them, very
conscious of the man beside her, a slight breeze ruffling
his dark hair and stirring the open collar of his shirt.
Nearer than the other scents, she was suddenly keenly
aware of the clean smell of his cotton shirt, the heavier
one of the denim jacket, and a faint, fresh scent that had
a uniquely male quality.

A few more people gathered on the wharf. Turning,
Jacinth saw that someone was selling fish from one of the
containers unloaded from the boat.

Mark said, "Hang on a minute," and left her side to
join the small knot of people. He came back with a par-
cel wrapped in newspaper.

"Do you like fish?" he asked.

"Yes."

"I got us one each," he said. "And a small one for Hecate."

"They're not cleaned, are they?" she said, hesitating.

"I'll do it, if you'll cook them. Is it a deal?" He was grinning, his head to one side, his eyebrows raised.

She said, since he had left her little choice, "All right. Are you a fisherman?"

"Not really, but I've been fishing with friends in the islands. You soon learn how to prepare your own catch. Coming?" he asked, and they stepped back over the uneven planks of the wharf to the road. "Hold on," Mark said. "I'll take this back to the car."

She waited, and when he rejoined her, his mouth quirking in a smile, she smiled back, feeling suddenly light and carefree.

He slipped an arm about her shoulders, companionably, and she was surprised to find that she liked it, the casual embrace giving her an unaccustomed sensation of being warmed and protected.

Past the shops were a few houses, tucked among windswept trees, and climbing up a steep, bush-covered slope on the other side of the road. A faded notice at the entrance to a worn dirt path read "Lookout," and Mark said, "Are you game to climb up to the bluff?"

"Yes, of course."

"Come on then." He took her hand as they crossed the road, waiting for a large truck to rumble past, laden with sheep and leaving behind an odour that was even stronger than the fish on the wharf. But as they began to climb the path, the pungent farm smell receded and was replaced by the pleasant tang of small-leaved manuka that grew shoulder-high on either side. He let her set the pace, and when the path narrowed, dropped behind. At a steep part

there were a dozen or so steps cut into the sandstone, and
Mark said, "Want me to go first?"

Jacinth shook her head, hitching her skirt a little because it was too tight fitting to allow her much freedom
of movement. When the track resumed she turned in
well-hidden triumph, and found that he was still standing at the bottom of the steps, on his face a narrow-eyed
look of frank appreciation. Quickly she turned and
walked away, glad that the exertion of climbing gave her
a good excuse for the heat in her cheeks when he caught
up with her.

At the top was a grassy, flat area, with a wooden seat
overlooking the sea. Panting slightly, Jacinth subsided
onto it, and Mark, slipping off his jacket, grinned down
at her. "You're out of condition," he scoffed.

"Probably. It's a lovely view, isn't it?"

It was, a sweeping view of the boats gently rocking at
their moorings, the island, covered in scrub down to the
waterline and looking completely untouched, the settle-
ments nestled into neighbouring bays, and the arms of
the little harbour curving in the distance to the gap that
led to the open sea. The road wound round the foot of
the bluff, and although they couldn't see them, the sound
of cars sweeping round the curve came clearly up the
steep slope.

Mark walked to the low fence that marked the edge of
the bluff, and stood for a while with his jacket slung on
his shoulder, then turned, flung the jacket over the back
of the seat, and sat down with his arm resting on top of
it, behind Jacinth.

She knew when he stopped admiring the view and
turned to look at her, instead. Resolutely, she gave no
sign that she had noticed.

His hand moved from behind her, and lightly he
brushed the back of his fingers up the side of her neck
from her collar, to her jawline and her cheek.

Jacinth stiffened automatically. "Don't," she said, distantly.

His fingers stilled, then fell away, returning to the seat back by her shoulder. "You're very like Hecate, aren't you?" he said. "Only I have a feeling that if I wait for you to make the approach, I'll wait until doomsday."

She kept on staring at the view as though she hadn't heard, her heart beating suffocatingly, everything in her tense and desperately aware of him. She should get up and walk away.

His hand moved again to her shoulder, and the fingers of his other hand came firmly under her chin, turning her to face him. His eyes were bright, intent, the message in them unmistakable. "Well," he said lightly, "if the mountain won't—"

"Don't flirt with me, Mark," she said, trying to move from his hold, but his fingers tightened, and the brightness in his eyes changed to a hard, almost angry light.

"I'm not flirting," he said, and he lifted her face until her mouth met his.

Jacinth had braced herself, knowing what was coming, but she wasn't prepared for the devastating shock of sheer pleasure she experienced. She tried to grasp his wrist in protest, but he pulled her hand away, holding it down in her lap, his other arm about her shoulders, bringing her closer to him.

Her mouth opened helplessly under his, although her body was still rigid with tension. He released her hand, and she felt his fingers caressing her arched throat, then curving round it, his thumb finding the slight hollow at its base. His hand slid down, inside the open jacket, and his palm covered her breast.

Jacinth felt a slow, hot tide flow through her as he gently stroked the softness under his hand. Then Mark's tongue was in her mouth, and she was going dizzy with a whole lot of utterly new, explosive sensations.

Her body, of its own volition, made a shivering, blind adjustment, her head shifting slightly under the assault of his mouth, her waist yielding to aid the exploration of his hand.

And then she heard the voices of people climbing the path, and in sudden panic wrenched herself out of his arms and stood, her breathing quick and agitated.

Mark cursed under his breath and wiped a hand over his face, looking flushed and slightly dazed. A couple and two children emerged from the scrub, and Jacinth, without looking back, rushed past them to the path and plunged down the slope.

Mark didn't catch up until she had nearly reached the road. "What's the hurry?" he said, sounding amused. If he had been at all disconcerted, he had quickly regained his composure.

When she didn't answer, he said, "They couldn't have seen anything, you know. And if they had, it wouldn't matter. We weren't exactly *in flagrante*."

She felt a flush rise to her cheeks, and hurried more, almost running out of the trees, her momentum carrying her to the edge of the road as a car came round the corner of the bluff.

"*Watch out!*" Hard fingers clamped about her arm, and Mark hauled her back, jerking her against him. "What are you doing?" he demanded, holding her away from him, his grip still painful.

She said, sharply, "I had stopped. Let go."

His fingers relaxed their hold, and she said with faint sarcasm, "Thank you."

Mark was still frowning. "Are you all right?"

"Yes, of course." She was regathering her customary air of indifference, wrapping it about her like a protective cloak. Carefully she looked both ways, then stepped out onto the road. She walked quickly back to the car, with Mark keeping pace beside her in grim silence. He

opened the passenger door for her, casting her a puzzled, searching glance as she got in. He put the key in the
ignition, then gave a sharp sigh, and raised his hand to
turn her head as he had on the bluff. "What's the matter, Jacinth?" he asked.

"Nothing." Her eyes were stony, blank. She was hiding a strange kind of panic, afraid of him, of her own
emotions, of what he could do to them, turning them
upside down in minutes.

"That's not true," he said. "Is it? Jacinth—" He
gripped her shoulders with both hands, and his lips
brushed her forehead, her cheek.

In a hard little voice she said, "Don't. Don't touch
me."

His head went back, but his hands still gripped.
"What?"

"You heard." Her eyes met his, cold, defiant.

Mark's mouth tightened. "Ten minutes ago you didn't
seem to mind."

"I said, if you remember, the same thing then."

"And didn't mean it," he accused.

"Are you one of those men who can't believe it when
a woman says no?" she asked, with stinging sarcasm. "I
said, *don't touch me!* I meant it then, and I mean it now.
So take your hands *off* me, Mark!"

Slowly he moved his hands, his eyes not leaving her
face. "You little hypocrite," he said. "You may have
been as stiff as a board, and I'd love to know the reason
why, but your *mouth* was telling me a different story,
darling, and very eloquently, too. And just before we
were so rudely interrupted, do you think I didn't feel you
suddenly cave in? For a minute, there, you were all mine,
Jacinth, and don't think I didn't know it."

"You're imagining things."

His breath hissed through his teeth. "I'm tempted to
make you take that back, here and now."

"You dare!"

Their eyes clashed. He said, "I'd dare, all right. And pretty soon, I'll damn well do it, too. But right now I'm so angry, I don't trust myself not to hurt you. And believe it or not, that *isn't* what I want."

He turned away from her and started the car. Jacinth, making an effort to breathe slowly and evenly, sat with her hands clasped and her back very, very straight. After half an hour, she took out her bag, and turning away from him as far as she could, renewed her lipstick. Mark didn't comment, or look at her, but a fleeting glance showed her the slight, sardonic curving of his mouth. She took her eyes away and resolutely stared out the window.

CHAPTER ELEVEN

WHEN the car stopped outside her house, Jacinth said, "Thank you. You don't need to come in."

"Yes, I do," Mark told her.

She drew in a quick breath, ready to protest, and he said, "The fish, remember? We had a deal."

"You're welcome to it. I really don't want—"

"You wouldn't deprive Hecate of her dinner, would you?"

"Oh, stop it, Mark! You know perfectly well—"

"No," he interrupted harshly. "I *don't* know. I don't know what made you suddenly change—"

"I haven't changed."

"*You changed*. For a while today you acted like a flesh and blood woman—warm and friendly and even passionate. And then you turned into the original ice-maiden again. Is that what you did to Philip? Switched it on and off for him like a light? No wonder he looked so bewildered."

She cast him a look of freezing scorn, and pushed open her door, slamming it behind her.

He was at her side in a flash, catching at her arm as she tried to pass. "Don't, Jacinth," he said. "I don't want to fight with you."

Her face fixed in its customary smooth mask, she said, "I'm not fighting. It's been a long day, and I'd like to go inside, if you don't mind."

Her voice was exquisitely polite. Briefly, his hand tightened on her arm, and his eyes darkened. But after a moment he released his hold. With deceptive gentleness, he said, "All right, we'll play it your way, for now. Let me come in, Jacinth. I promise I won't try to force my unwelcome attentions on you, OK? I'll clean the fish, and we'll cook it and have a meal together. And then I'll go. Promise."

She looked at him searchingly. "Sweet-talking?" she enquired ironically, and he laughed.

"If you like. But I really would like to share this fish with you, Jacinth. And I don't make a habit of leaping on unwilling women. Trust me."

She didn't trust him an inch, but she found herself saying, "Come in, then. Hecate will be glad to see you—when she finds you bearing her gifts."

Hecate fell enthusiastically on her fish. Mark efficiently cleaned and scaled the other two, and Jacinth left them marinating in white wine and herbs, and suggested a predinner drink. While inwardly she was shaken and confused, to Mark she presented her usual manner of controlled calm, and was determined to let nothing ruffle it. She passed Mark his drink and sank gracefully into her chair with her own glass in her hand, prepared to make meaningless small talk.

Mark followed her lead with impeccable courtesy, but increasingly she gained an impression that he was hiding an angry frustration, and her remarks became more and more stilted and forced. Finally she made an excuse that she must see to the dinner, and fled to the kitchen.

She was peeling potatoes at the sink when Hecate came in and began rubbing about her legs. Looking down, she said bitterly, "Yes, that's all very well, but you gave in to *him* first, didn't you?"

Hecate sat down at her feet, the pupils of her unblinking eyes narrowed to black slits. Jacinth said, "*You* may have fallen for his sweet-talk, but I'm damned if *I* will."

Hecate cocked her head to one side, enquiringly.

Jacinth said under her breath, "Oh, he's sitting in there as though butter wouldn't melt, but he's furious, really, biding his time. The 'no woman is going to get the better of me' syndrome. He thinks I've rejected him. Well, so I have, and he'd better just get used to the idea."

Hecate lifted a hind leg and began assiduously washing herself.

"You wait," Jacinth said darkly. "He'd like to have us both eating out of his hand. Well, I for one am not falling for it."

As she was putting the potatoes on the stove, Mark wandered in. "Can I be of any help?"

"No, thanks," she answered crisply.

"Pour you another drink, then?"

"No. Perhaps later, when we're eating. Have another yourself, if you'd like."

He shook his head. "I'll be driving home afterwards."

She almost retorted that she was relieved to hear it, but bit back the provocative remark. She hoped he would take the hint and go back to the living room, but he continued to lean in the doorway, watching her, until in desperation she suggested he should set the table in the dining room.

He made a good job of it. When she saw that he had taken the branched candlestick from the sideboard and placed it on the table, she stopped short in the doorway, holding the two plates of fish dished up with buttered potatoes, peas and carrots. He had lit the candles but had not turned on the light, and the soft glow created an intimate setting for two among the shadows of the room.

He came over and took the plates to put them on the table, pulling out a chair for her and waiting expectantly.

She could switch on the light, but that would look rather silly, she supposed. Instead, she let him seat her, and waited for him to take the chair opposite hers.

"It looks delicious," he said. "I see Nadine has passed on her talent for cooking."

"I'm not up to my mother's standard, I'm afraid. In anything."

He glanced at her sharply, in the act of picking up his fork. "She is very—talented in the domestic arts. I have the idea that your gifts lie in other directions."

"Yes." She turned her attention to the fish. She didn't want to start discussing her mother.

Mark did the dishes while Jacinth made coffee. When they carried their cups into the lounge, Hecate was on one of the armchairs, curled into a tight black ball with her tail over her nose. She opened one eye suspiciously, and Jacinth said, "You're not supposed to sit there, cat."

The eye closed disdainfully. Mark chuckled. "She's not doing any harm."

"My mother would be horrified."

He waited until she had taken the other armchair, then sat on the sofa. "Your mother doesn't live here any more," he reminded her.

"The house is still hers."

He looked about the room. Except for the fact that Nadine had removed several of her favourite ornaments and pictures, the room was the same as it had been the first time he had been in it. "Yes," he said. "You're not much like her, are you?"

Jacinth sensed a criticism in the words. "I take after my father, I suppose," she said. "Although apparently he was dark."

"I didn't mean in looks."

She hadn't supposed he did. But it seemed safer to assume that. "Well," she said, "I don't know much about him, except that he was obviously unreliable."

Mark cradled his cup in his hand. "He was only one man, Jacinth."

"What do you mean?"

"That you shouldn't tar us all with the same brush, perhaps."

"You're jumping to conclusions, aren't you?"

"I guess so. How *do* you feel about men in general, Jacinth?" he asked bluntly.

"As you just pointed out," she rejoined coolly, "it doesn't do to generalise."

He inclined his head, conceding the point, and drank some more of his coffee.

When he got up to go, she quickly rose, too. Hecate stirred on her chair, sat up and yawned. Mark stretched out a hand and stroked the cat's sleek head. "Goodnight, Hecate," he said. She bowed her head submissively to his hand, shifted her haunches and purred.

Jacinth looked on, exasperated. Mark straightened. "Well, at least *she's* stopped treating me like Ivan the Terrible," he remarked.

"*I* can't be bought with fish," Jacinth said scathingly.

He laughed, passing her on his way to the door. "It wasn't the fish that did it," he said. "And I wouldn't dream of trying to buy you, Jacinth." He opened the front door himself, and looked back at her, still standing near the door of the lounge. "Sweet dreams," he said, and his eyes slipped over her, lingeringly. She had a sudden searing memory of his hand on her breast. For a long moment he held her eyes, and unmistakably, he was remembering, too.

"Goodnight," he said softly, and closed the door.

* * *

On Friday she was relieved to find that Mark had reverted to his usual office manner. Either he had decided to accept that she had no interest in a deeper relationship with him, or he was keeping their business life totally separate from any more personal feelings that might have developed between them.

But on Saturday he turned up while she was visiting her mother and Lyle. She had been asked by Nadine to deliver some more things from the house, and was invited to join them for lunch. Mark said he had just called to return some tools he had borrowed from his father, and wasn't staying, but Nadine insisted that he join them, and laid an extra place at the table for him.

When the meal was over, Jacinth picked up some dishes, and Mark followed her into the kitchen with some more. He stood beside her as she packed plates into the dishwasher.

"I can manage," she said.

"I know." He passed her another plate. "You should learn to accept help gracefully."

"And you should learn not to give people gratuitous advice."

"How about having dinner with me tonight?"

"No, thanks. I've already had one meal out today."

"Tomorrow night, then?"

Jacinth shook her head.

"Any night?" he asked dryly.

She carefully rinsed tea leaves out of a cup and placed it on the rack in the machine. "I don't think so, thank you."

"Do you mind telling me why?"

"I just don't think it's a good idea."

"Why not?"

Jacinth sighed. "For one thing, we work together. I've had one experience of a social relationship interfering with my job."

"You already have a social relationship with me," he pointed out. "Our parents are married to each other. So you can't very well cut me out of your private life. And I don't think it's escaped your notice that I've been careful to maintain a strictly business attitude to you at work."

Of course she had noticed. "I still don't think it's a good idea to be—close—outside working hours."

"What you're saying probably makes some sense," he admitted, and Jacinth said, "Well, then . . ."

"But I get the distinct feeling that you're making excuses."

Carefully she slid the last plate into the rack. Turning to face him, she said, "Sorry, but that's how I feel."

"I'd begun to think that it's your ambition not to feel a damn thing."

"If that remark is supposed to mean something—"

"It means that I'm curious as to why you backed off so fast after that kiss the other day."

"Oh, really, Mark! It was only a kiss." She made her voice lightly contemptuous.

"Exactly." He stood in her way as she turned toward the door. "So why have I suddenly become public enemy number one? It isn't as though I tried to rape you, or something."

"I'm sure you'd never do anything of the kind."

"No, I wouldn't," he said quietly. "Which is one reason I think you owe me some honesty."

"I don't owe you a thing," she said clearly. "You have no claims on me, Mark, so lay off, will you?"

"Am I crowding you?"

"*Yes.*"

She was staring into his eyes, her face chilly and hostile. Mark stared back at her steadily, a faint line between his brows, his eyes narrowed.

Then he raised his hands in a gesture of surrender, and took a step backwards. "OK. OK. I'll try to give you room. But I'm not giving up, Jacinth."

Inside her, a coldness gathered, like fear. Giving up on what? "What do you want from me?"

"I'll tell you," he said slowly. "I want to know what makes you tick, what's really inside that lovely shell you present to the world. The brutal truth is, I want to kiss you again, the way I did two days ago, and feel you respond as you did then—for all of two seconds. And then, I want to go on from there."

He held her mesmerised with his eyes, and something small and terrified inside her trembled.

"No," she whispered, her throat drying. "No."

"Oh, yes," he said, quietly confident. "Some day."

"Never!"

He smiled, a sudden light in his eyes. "You shouldn't challenge me, Jacinth. I never could resist a dare."

Nadine came into the kitchen, carrying the butter dish and a bowl of sugar. "Oh, you've finished? Thank you both so much. I must say, Mark, your father has you well trained."

"Actually, it was my mother's doing," Mark told her.

A frown crossed Nadine's face, and Mark said swiftly, "I'm sorry, would you rather we didn't mention my mother?"

"Oh, it's silly of me to be sensitive about it." Nadine grimaced. "But I can't seem to help it." She laid a hand on his arm. "Never mind, Mark, I know you didn't mean to be hurtful. Now, I came to tell you two that we're having our first real dinner party. We've just been planning it, and both of you must come. Not a big crowd, just a few friends, and our family. It *will* be rather special, though," she added, turning to Jacinth. "So do dress up, darling. You could wear your bridesmaid's dress.

Perhaps Mark will pick you up. You don't want to get
your clothes all crushed, driving yourself."

"I won't—" Jacinth started.

And Mark said, "Yes, of course. It's on my way. What
night?"

She told him, taking it for granted that they would
both be available, and shepherded them back into the
lounge to join Lyle. To refuse to go with Mark after that
would have been to make a big issue of a trivial proposal, and Jacinth resigned herself to having to accept his
escort. Not for the first time, she wondered if her mother
was indulging in a little matchmaking.

The dinner party was a credit to Nadine, who was in
her element playing hostess. Jacinth had been duly collected by Mark, and her mother welcomed them both
with a kiss, ran an expert eye over Jacinth's slim-fitting
black silk dress, which was dramatic with her fair col-
ouring, and said, "I thought you might wear the dress
you had for the wedding, but that's very nice, dear. The
gold bracelets do dress it up quite well."

"She looks almost as beautiful as her mother," Lyle
said. "Come on, what can I pour for you, Jacinth?"

"I'll fix her drink, Dad," Mark offered as the door-
bell announced other guests arriving. He hadn't commented on Jacinth's appearance, but now he flicked an
appraising glance over her and said, "My father is bi-
ased."

Darrel was there already, welcoming Jacinth with a kiss
and a compliment, and showing a distinct propensity to
stay by her side. Mark and he exchanged a few teasing
remarks, before Nadine called on Jacinth to help her
hand around some pre-dinner hors d'oeuvres.

At dinner, Jacinth unexpectedly found herself a centre of interest. Most of the dozen guests were friends of
Lyle's, and Nadine seemed anxious to show off her

daughter to them, and to enumerate her accomplishments. "Jacinth is a qualified accountant, would you believe? And I can barely even add two and two!" Then, later, "Jacinth was always such a tall girl—someone told me she should have been a model. Of course, it was dreadful for her when she was younger—the tallest girl in the school when she was twelve, and towering over the boys—so embarrassing for a girl at that age. Wasn't it, darling? But I told her she was lucky, really. I've always had trouble getting clothes to fit properly, being small. Especially shoes! Size three are almost impossible to find. Of course, Jacinth is a perfectly normal five.... Jacinth lived at home, you know, until I married Lyle. We've always been close. I hope you're not missing me too badly, darling? Jacinth may be a career girl, but I'm sure she'll never be *hard*.... Do you know, Jacinth says she isn't interested in marriage, but I told her, when the right man comes along, she'll change her mind. I know I shouldn't say it, but she's really a very pretty girl."

Jacinth, trying to turn the conversation, found an unexpected and unobtrusive ally in Mark. She thought the look he flashed her held a certain amount of sympathy, before he followed up on some random remark of hers, and skilfully steered the talk into other channels.

Driving her home, he said, "Your mother embarrassed you tonight, didn't she?"

"Slightly," Jacinth acknowledged, not wanting to admit how deeply uncomfortable she had really been. She knew that Nadine meant well, and she didn't want to imply any criticism of her mother.

"You hid it well," Mark said, in a rather strange voice. "Most people wouldn't have guessed."

"Good."

He flicked a glance at her, then returned his eyes to the road. A little later, he said, "You're not pretty, you know."

She turned her head to look at him, surprised.

Slanting her a grin, he added, "Beautiful, yes. Lovely, I'd pass. But not pretty."

"Do I say thank you?"

He laughed. "Only if you want to."

She looked away in silence, and after a few seconds he laughed again, softly, and didn't speak until he drew the car up outside her gate.

He turned to her then, and asked, "Would you mind if I kissed you goodnight?"

"Yes, I would."

She reached for the handle of the door, and he said, "Why?"

"Do I need a reason?" Her hand on the latch, she turned to face him.

"I think so, yes."

"I'm not in the habit of paying for the ride, when someone offers me a lift."

He didn't move, but she knew that he was angry. "Below the belt, Jacinth," he said. "You know perfectly well I wasn't asking for payment."

Stonily, she insisted, "That's what it sounded like."

He rested his arm on the steering wheel, looking at her thoughtfully. Slowly, he said, "I think I'm beginning to understand you, Jacinth."

Her heart lurched in fright. Snapping open the door, she said, "I certainly hope so. I don't think I can spell it out any more clearly. When I say I don't want to be kissed, *I don't want to be kissed.*"

"Okay," he said, as she gracefully swung her legs out of the car. "I've got that message, loud and clear. But it wasn't what I meant."

She stood up and closed the door behind her. But of course, he got out, too, and followed her up the path. He waited while she unlocked the door and opened it. Hecate bounded up the steps from out of the shadows and brushed by her legs. Without looking at Mark, Jacinth said, "Goodnight, and thanks for the lift."

His hand on her arm pulled her round, and for a long moment his mouth was hard and warm on hers. She barely had time to lift a hand in protest before she was free again, and Mark said, with a disconcerting hint of laughter in his voice, "Goodnight, little cat."

She switched on the light and slammed the door.

Hecate wound around her ankles, purring, then sat down a few feet away and looked up at her.

"Yes, well, I don't think he meant you," Jacinth told her.

Hecate blinked, and Jacinth said, "I saw you stalking that bird this morning. Mark's got the same look in his eye."

Hecate made a little sound of protest, rising from her haunches, her tail waving from side to side.

"Oh, yes, he has," Jacinth said. "I don't care what you say. Something about me has aroused his hunting instincts. He wants to know what makes me tick—I bet he took all his toys apart when he was a little boy, and probably pulled the wings off flies and dissected frogs. Now he's interested in finding out how *people* work. I've become some kind of challenge to him. The way he looks at me is the way Ed Hillary must have looked at Everest."

And Everest had been conquered. Jacinth shivered.

CHAPTER TWELVE

WINTER was coming on, the days growing chilly. When Mark said, "How do you fancy a few days in the islands?" Jacinth thought he was joking.

But apparently he was quite serious. "There are changes pending in the company, especially with the planned expansion into our own trade shops for crafts and nonperishable goods, and they want some representation from the New Zealand side at the Annual General Meeting. It's planned to take place before the AGM here, so that we can report back to our local shareholders."

"We?"

"I'll be attending, and now that we have one, they expect the company secretary to be there, too."

"Oh."

"Oh? I expected more enthusiasm for an all-expenses-paid jaunt into the tropics, at this time of the year."

"It's not a holiday, is it?"

"Certainly not. We'll be working quite hard, but not for twenty-four hours a day, I hope. Have you ever been to the Cook Islands?"

"No. I believe they're very beautiful."

Beautiful was an understatement, she discovered.

Having left Auckland just after midday on Tuesday, Mark and Jacinth had crossed the date line during the flight, and arrived at Rarotonga on the evening of the day before. After being waved through the customs area by a smiling Cook Islander they were met by another, who placed leis of sweet smelling white frangipani about their necks, and embraced Mark enthusiastically. He was a tall, big-built man with an expansive grin and a tight mat of black curls cut very short. He wore a spanking white shirt, a purple-and-white flowered *pareu* tied about his ample waist, and brown leather sandals on his broad feet.

Mark said, "Jacinth, this is my friend, Turangahakoa Avana."

"Call me Tu," the big islander invited, enveloping her hand in a large brown one. "So you're our new company secretary, eh?"

"Yes."

"*Kia orana*, Jacinth. Welcome to our island."

The greeting, meaning "May you live," was one she was to hear often in the next few days.

The modest hotel where they stayed was on the beach front, their rooms individual little bungalows set among tall palms and wide lawns. It was dark when they arrived, and although she could see little, the sound of the sea and the white glimmer of the waves breaking on the reef tantalized her.

Tu had said he would wait in the hotel bar for Mark; the two men intended to have a business discussion as soon as Mark had settled into his room.

"Do you want me in on your meeting with Tu?" Jacinth asked Mark before entering her bungalow.

"If you feel up to it. You won't need to take notes, but it might help you to understand what goes on at the meeting tomorrow."

"Don't wait for me," she said, "but I'll come along when I've unpacked a few things."

Finding the temperature much warmer than back home, she changed from her blouse and skirt into a pink cotton dress with a minimal top that tied on the shoulders. When she joined the men, they had procured a supper of sandwiches and tropical fruits. Jacinth wasn't very hungry, but she had a banana and then, sipping a glass of freshly squeezed pineapple juice, sat and listened carefully.

As their talk concluded, Tu said, "You two must come and eat with my family one night, before you go home."

Mark thanked him and promised to take him up on the invitation.

After Tu had left them, Mark said, "I'll be taking a stroll on the beach before turning in. Care to join me?"

"Sounds good," she murmured. "I'd like that."

He looked critically at her cotton dress and sandals. "You might want a cardigan. And some walking shoes. Something closed in. You did bring some?"

Jacinth nodded. He had warned her when they discussed the trip that she would need them. "The sand is crushed coral," he had said, "and the bits that aren't completely broken down yet can be sharp. It pays to be careful, because coral cuts go septic very quickly."

She put on a pair of synthetic-soled canvas flatties. He glanced at them approvingly and took her arm. He had changed his shoes too, and with his khaki shirt and trousers was wearing a pair of sneakers that had definitely seen better days.

They talked about the company as they strolled along the quiet beach. There were lights moving out in the dark water, and Mark said they would be islanders fishing. They met a young couple with their arms about each other, looking dreamy and happy. Mark hadn't attempted to take Jacinth's hand, and they walked a foot apart. The water rippled quietly at their feet, and the boom of the waves on the reef that protected the beach came clearly across the tranquil, sheltered lagoon. After a while they stopped talking, enjoying the peaceful atmosphere, the starry sky, the sound of the breeze stirring the palm leaves.

Eventually they retraced their steps and crossed sparse, sandy grass to the hotel. Mark opened the door of her bungalow for her, and brushed his lips across her temple as she turned to go inside. "Goodnight, Jacinth," he said.

"Goodnight, Mark." She turned to him, and he bent again, and just touched her lips with his mouth, before she stepped back and rather quickly closed the door.

As she stumbled into bed, she found herself stupidly smiling.

In daylight, Jacinth was enchanted by the clear blue water, the classic white sand and palm trees fringing the lagoon, the steep, heavily tree-covered mountains of the interior. The whole place looked a picture-postcard tropical paradise.

They breakfasted on papaya, fresh citrus juice and rolls, and then took a hired car to the centre of Avarua.

The capital was a large, busy town, but even here the tropics cast their spell. Houses and shops were set among palm trees swaying in a perpetual balmy breeze. There were no high-rise buildings. "Nothing taller than a palm tree," Mark told her. "It's an unwritten law." The air was languidly warm, the streets hummed with the musical language of Polynesia, and the bright flowered prints worn by men and women alike added more than a hint of local colour. Some of the men unselfconsciously sported a brilliant hibiscus flower behind one ear, others a garland of frangipani or scarlet ginger flowers atop their tight, crisp curls. Women decorated their glossy black hair with flowers, too, or wore hats fashioned of fragrant blossoms or green leaves.

Mark led the way to an unpretentious building with Pacific Trade Enterprises painted on a board beside the doorway.

The Annual General Meeting was held in a large, airy boardroom hung with beautifully patterned dyed tapa cloth. Mark had warned Jacinth that here business was

conducted in a rather different manner from the way
things were done back home. The meeting occupied two
days, and there seemed to be no hurry. Long and repeti-
tive speeches were listened to without any sign of impatience, although sometimes Jacinth suspected that a few
in the audience were indulging in a quiet nap.

On Tuesday evening, Jacinth felt very tired. Mark
seemed to be immune to such weakness.

"Tomorrow Tu is taking us in a car round the island," he told her, "with stops at the villages along the
way to see the goods we hope to sell in the craft shops.
We'll be ordering some, now that we have the go-ahead
for the idea. Would you like to have dinner out tonight?"

"No, thank you. I'm tired," she confessed. The last
two days had been interesting but a strain, and she
couldn't help but find that having two Mondays in the
week was not only strange but in some way exhausting,
as well.

He looked at her with a sceptical glint in his eyes, but
accepted the excuse. "Right," he said. "You do look a
bit weary, at that. The worst is over, though. You'll enjoy yourself tomorrow."

Going round the island was a twenty-five-mile drive on
a flat road, but with side trips up short, steep tracks into
hills planted with bananas, citrus and breadfruit trees, it
took the whole day. The houses were virtually all tin-
roofed, modest wooden bungalows. There were very few
palm-thatched dwellings left on the island. Durable and
easy-to-use corrugated iron was no doubt more convenient, Jacinth thought, though less picturesque. The sur-
rounding gardens, lush with glossy-leaved trees, and
flowers ranging from white through to the brilliant scarlet of the hibiscus hedges and ginger flowers, softened the
effect. Many of the homes had carefully tended graves in
their front yards.

"Rarotongans are close to their forebears," Tu explained. "Living or dead, it is all one family. When my grandfather feels lonely for my grandmother, he goes out in the night and talks to her. Sometimes he sleeps on her grave."

They looked at village crafts of the type that Mark hoped to sell at the company's projected retail outlets in New Zealand: woven mats with patterned borders, tapa cloth, lovely appliquéd *ti vaevae* work, palm baskets, and the exquisitely fashioned, palest cream, finely woven hats for which the Cooks were famous. "We will make sure we have some hats from Penrhyn Island, for the shops," Tu said. "That's where the finest hats are made."

"But these are quite beautiful!" Jacinth said. Seduced by their elegance, she bought one, and wore it for the rest of her stay.

At the last village, when evening was on its way, they were given a meal of pork, taro and boiled green bananas, and entertained with dancing. Half a dozen girls in long hula-style skirts made not of grass, Tu told Jacinth, but the fibres from the *puro* tree, swayed gracefully in the gathering dusk in the traditional style that Jacinth had seen often enough in films and television programmes. Sitting beside Mark on a coconut fibre mat, she found the swish of the girls' skirts and the graceful waving of their arms, accompanied by the peculiarly sweet tones of Polynesian singing, strangely moving. The real thing was so much more romantic than watching a filmed performance, however polished.

"Our dancers are famous throughout the Pacific," Tu told her proudly. "Even better than the Tahitians."

The men joined in a couple of the dances, stomping their feet and moving their hips to the sound of a hollow wooden slit drum. The last item was the famous lovedance of the Pacific, the *tamure*. The drumbeat quick and insistent, the girls' hips rotating faster and faster, the men advancing and retreating, bending their knees and moving them rhythmically in invitation to their partners. People from the audience were getting up and joining in, and others were clapping and laughing, urging on the dancers.

Mark said in her ear, "You haven't lived until you've seen a Cook Islands *tamure*." He laughed softly. "Captain Cook and his officers were shocked to the back teeth by it."

Jacinth could see why. It was certainly uninhibited, the smiling dancers blending innocent fun and frank sensuality in a way that was enormously seductive.

A girl with laughing dark eyes moved over to them, her hands on her gyrating hips, and danced in front of Tu, obviously inviting him to partner her. Tu leaped to his feet and accepted the challenge, and Mark said to Jacinth, "Care to try it?"

She shook her head. "I wouldn't have the faintest clue how. I'd rather watch. Thanks, anyway."

"Chicken," he said, but didn't press her, and when one of the women invited him to join her, he smilingly declined. Soon the drumbeat stopped, and the dancers stood panting and happy, or subsided laughing onto the mats spread on the ground.

The following day Tu and Mark conferred again about the supplies of handicrafts, and had to see some other people concerning a transportation problem. Jacinth shopped in Avarua, buying duty-free perfume and a necklet of island cultured pearls for her mother. Tu had recommended the Women's Craft Centre, and she spent some time there, and bought a beautiful appliquéd bedspread with matching pillow covers.

In the afternoon she swam in the lagoon, sharing the beach with several tourists and a party of laughing brown children who arrived riding bareback on two sleepy-looking horses. The water was shallow and very clear, the sand littered with spotted sea slugs. "Don't worry about them," Mark had told her when she mentioned her plans. "But wear something on your feet. If you stand on a stonefish, which is practically invisible until you do, you can get badly hurt. And there's always the danger of sharp coral."

That evening they had dinner with Tu, his wife Tiari and their family of five children.

Tiari served them traditional food including marinated raw fish, taro with its spinachlike leaves cooked in coconut milk, and breadfruit. Tu's plump, black-eyed children seemed at first in awe of the visitors, but by the end of the evening the youngest was sitting on Jacinth's lap, and the next one leaned against her knee, gazing into her face and reaching up a hand to touch her hair. Tu's wife, dressed in a *pareu* tied over her breasts to fall in graceful folds, whispered to Mark, and when he nodded and said, "Ask her," she turned to Jacinth.

"I would like to give you a present, Jacinth," she said.

Having been told not to give tips or presents because custom demanded a gift in return, Jacinth glanced at Mark.

"Tiari has a *pareu* for you," he said. "Perhaps you'd like to send her some small thing from New Zealand, after you get home."

"Yes, of course." She turned to Tiari, smiling her thanks. "I hope that it looks as good on me as yours does on you."

"Come with me," the woman said. "I'll show you how to tie it."

In the bedroom, she presented a length of flower-printed blue cotton, and Jacinth learned how to tie a firm knot and anchor the ends so that there was no chance of modesty being endangered. Infected by Tiari's giggles as she showed her how to do it, she was soon flushed with laughter herself, and although for a moment she balked at walking into the other room to let the men see how she looked, she didn't have the heart to refuse when Tiari so obviously wanted to show her off.

Tu and the children clapped their hands. Mark, smiling broadly, took a hibiscus flower from a small vase standing on the table and tucked it behind her right ear.

Tu suddenly snatched up a small slit drum that stood in a corner of the room, and began beating on it, a clacking rhythm that Jacinth recognised as the *tamure*.

Mark, it seemed, had been hiding his light under a bushel. He pushed the table into a corner and turned to Jacinth. His eyes daring her, he spread his arms out and began to dance, inviting her to follow. Obviously, he was quite practised.

"Oh, no!" she said, laughing. "I don't know how."

"We'll show you!" Tiari insisted, and began to move her hips fluidly from side to side. "Look, like this!"

Jacinth shook her head, but Mark said quietly, "It's not that hard; don't be a spoilsport. A child can do it."

The children were dancing, too, even the two-year-old weaving her plump hands and moving her hips almost in time to the beat.

It turned into a most extraordinary evening. The family's high spirits and friendliness infected Jacinth with a zest for life and a reckless happiness that she had never known. She followed Tiari self-consciously at first, and then with increasing confidence. She danced with one of the children, an eight-year-old boy who had her laughing with him the whole time, and then a slightly older boy beat the drum and Tu partnered Tiari, their movements faster and faster and increasingly erotic until Jacinth and Mark had to stop, panting and content to watch the superb exhibition their hosts were giving them.

When at last Mark suggested they should leave, she said, "I'll just go and change."

"Why?" he asked. "You look fine like that. A trifle
dishevelled," he added, reaching up to tuck a stray wisp
of her hair behind her ear. "But I must admit I like it."

She grimaced at him, and disappeared into the bedroom. She picked up her dress from the bed, but Mark
was right. There wasn't much point in changing, so she
rolled it up and stuffed it into the shoulder bag she had
brought, instead.

They had arrived in a hired car, and she put the bag on
the floor in front of her as she waved goodbye to Tu and
Tiari and the children who, except for the baby, had
shown no signs of being tired.

"Enjoy yourself?" Mark asked unnecessarily.

"You know I did," she answered. "They're wonderful people."

"Yes, I'm very fond of them both."

Jacinth shivered suddenly, and he ran a finger down
her arm. "Cold?"

"Not really. It's a bit cooler out here, though."

She was disconcerted by the reaction that light, casual
touch had woken in her. Suddenly she was on fire, remembering with astonishing clarity a certain kiss that had
taken place some weeks before. She bit down hard on her
lower lip, trying to bury the memory.

He stopped the car outside the hotel, and said, "I'm
going for a walk along the beach. Want to come?"

"It's dark," she said unconvincingly.

He laughed. "There's a moon. Do you want to end the
evening by going tamely to bed?"

She didn't, really. She felt keyed up and restless, and
knew she wouldn't sleep. A walk on the sand in the
moonlight would be a good way to wind down. But a
walk in the moonlight with Mark could hold its dangers.

He said softly, "Turn off the calculator, Jacinth."

"What?"

He raised his hand and lightly tapped her forehead with a finger. "That little machine you have in there, that adds up all the pros and cons before you make the smallest decision. Switch it off and do what your feelings tell you, for a change. You want to come, don't you?"

"I don't add up everything—"

"Yes, you do. It's second nature to you. Come on." He glanced down at her feet, encased in a pair of canvas flatties, got out of the car and walked round to open her door. "We're going for a walk."

He took her hand firmly in his and led her to the beach. The sand was cool and scrunched under their feet, the white line of the reef glimmered in the distance, and moonlight gilded the silken water of the lagoon.

They walked slowly and in silence, breathing in the scents of frangipani and salt water and coconut. The shimmering, indented shoreline seemed to beckon them on forever, but at last Mark said, "We should turn back."

"Yes," Jacinth said with a sigh. "I suppose."

He looked down at her, and smiled crookedly. His hand moved from hers and slid up her arm, closing gently on her shoulder as the thumb moved hypnotically over her cool skin. Jacinth stood very still, her eyes downcast.

"I want to kiss you," Mark said. "Properly. You know that, don't you?"

She didn't answer, and he said, "At least you've stopped jumping away every time I touch you. Look at me, Jacinth."

She stirred then, a slight movement of protest, but he grasped her other shoulder, pulling her toward him. "Look at me," he repeated.

Reluctantly, she raised her eyes to his face, saw his eyes darken, the pupils wide. She suddenly felt very warm, the blood pounding through her veins in the throbbing rhythm of the *tamure*. Her mouth parted slightly on a quickly indrawn breath, and then it was crushed and moulded under his, taken remorselessly in a kiss of fiery sweetness.

She yielded to him, her body curving against his arm, while his other hand roamed across the bare skin of her shoulders and back. Her hands were spread on his chest, her palm covering the beating of his heart; then she slid her arms around him.

When his mouth lifted from hers, she heard herself give a tiny, distant moan of distress, but he gathered her even closer and began pressing hot, brief kisses along her neck. He opened his mouth over the firm, smooth skin on the curve of her shoulder, and she felt the heat of his breath, the gentle scrape of his teeth on her skin.

Jacinth shivered, and he lifted his head again. "Did I hurt you?"

"No," she whispered. "No...but I...you shouldn't!"

She felt him give a soundless laugh, and suddenly her bones seemed to be melting inside her. "Darling," he said. "I want to eat the whole of you. I want—" He moved quite suddenly, standing with his legs apart, his hand shifting down her back to pull her against him.

Jacinth, her arms about his neck, swayed off balance, and Mark said roughly, *"I want you!"*

His hands moved to her hair, and she felt him removing the pins that held it confined, felt the slither of it falling against her shoulders, and his fingers touching its softness, caressing, finally tugging until her lips met his again, and crushing a handful in his fist as his mouth explored, demanded, begged....

She had never known it could be like this, a roaring tide of sensation, of heat and closeness and shuddering delight. Delight in giving, and taking, and sharing a passion that was mutual and all-consuming.

They swayed together until she lost her balance and fell
to the white sand, taking him with her, and he gave a low
exclamation, pressing her down beneath him, his hands
running over her body, mouth on the soft curve just
above the edge of her *pareu*, his weight crushing her until something dug into her bare skin just below her
shoulder blade, and she cried out with the sudden pain.

Mark's head lifted quickly. "What is it?"

"I don't know." She gasped, trying to sit up. "Something—it felt sharp. On my back." Her hands were on his
shoulders, her cheek against the slight roughness of his.

He sat up, pulling her with him. "I'm a fool," he said.
"I'm sorry, Jacinth. I should have remembered about the
coral. Let me see."

He tucked her head against him, holding it with his
hand under her tumbled hair, and said, "It's bleeding a
little. I'll take you back to the hotel and put some anti-
septic on for you."

He pressed his lips to her shoulder for a long, excru-
ciating moment, and then helped her to her feet. Hooking
his arm about her waist, he said, "All right?"

"Yes. It won't kill me. It's only a scratch, isn't it?"

"I guess so." He kissed her temple. "I could kick myself for letting it happen, though. I ought to know better."

"It's not your fault," she said. She was just as much
to blame, had been equally blind and deaf to everything
except what was happening between them. It was like
emerging from a dream; she felt light-headed and as
though the real world were still very far away.

Back at the hotel, he fetched her bag from the car, and
said, "Do you have any disinfectant?"

"Yes, I bought a little first-aid kit to travel with."

He smiled. "I might have known you'd come prepared for any emergency. You won't be able to reach the
cut yourself, though. I'll come in with you."

She found the kit where she had placed it in the drawer of the bedside table, and he took out the small bottle of yellow disinfectant and a cotton wool pad. "Turn around," he ordered.

"Shouldn't it be washed first?"

"I suppose so. You're all sandy, anyway." He put the bottle down again on the bedside table, and said, "You'd better have a shower. Need any help?"

His smiling question asked something else, too, and she avoided his eyes as she said, "No, thanks. I'll manage."

When Jacinth had sluiced off the sand, rinsing some out of her hair, too, and dried herself, she donned the *pareu* again. Fortunately the cut had bled only slightly, and the material wasn't stained.

She hesitated before opening the door of the bathroom, taking a deep breath. She had made the shower as brief as possible, and tried not to think of the man waiting for her in the bedroom. She had quickly towelled and combed her hair, but the damp tendrils lay on her neck. She looked at herself in the mirror, saw a face devoid of make-up, naked and curiously vulnerable. With shaking fingers she found a lipstick and quickly smoothed on some colour. There wasn't time for more. She would make it clear to Mark that she expected him to apply the disinfectant for her and then leave.

He was sitting on the wide double bed, leaning back against the headboard with his arms folded.

Jacinth hesitated in the doorway, and he smiled at her, a light in his eyes that she had not seen before. It held tenderness, and welcome, and something else she was afraid to acknowledge.

"Come here," he said, turning to pick up the cotton wool and the bottle, but without getting off the bed. He patted the mattress beside him, and Jacinth stiffly walked over and sat down, turning sideways so that he could see her back.

JACINTH   153

She felt the cool sting of the disinfectant, and he said,
"It's stopped bleeding. I don't think it needs a dress-
ing."

She said, "Thank you," and then caught her breath as
his fingers closed about her upper arms, and she felt the
warm slide of his mouth across the skin of her back.

"Mark..." she said huskily.

"Mmm?" He was pressing soft kisses over her shoulder blade, then down the skin over her spine.

"I don't think—"

He laughed softly. "Good. Don't." His hands shifted
and turned her into his arms, and at the same time he
pushed her down onto the bed, and leaned over her, his
eyes brilliant with an emotion that made something kick
in her stomach, her breath quickening while her own eyes
widened.

His fingers smoothed the damp hair away from her
face. He said slowly, "I have never seen you look so
beautiful."

Sidetracked in spite of herself, she protested, "I'm a
mess!"

He laughed. "Not you. Never." His mouth came
down, aiming for hers, and she held him off with her
hands against his shoulders.

"Mark—"

"You said that before."

"Please," she said. "Please, Mark. I—I don't know
if this is a good idea."

"Believe me, it's a terrific idea. Why don't you stop
analysing everything, and take what comes?" Patiently,
he removed her hands, holding them in his while he bent
and kissed her, gently, and then with overwhelming passion.

She was close to giving in, her mouth opening under
his onslaught, responding like a flower to the sun. But her
mind was still in control in the background, a small core

of resistance, so that at last she wrenched her mouth from his and turned her head aside, panting, "Mark—please don't crowd me. I don't know yet if I really want this!"

He took a deep, unsteady breath. His lips brushed her neck, and then he eased his hold on her and shifted away, just a little. "All right, sweetheart," he said slowly. "But promise me one thing."

She turned to look at him. "What?"

"That you won't try freezing me out again. I had begun to suspect that the ice-maiden act was just a cover-up. Now I know it. And you can't fool me any more. So don't try."

"I don't put on any act," she said. "It's not like that."

He smiled at her sceptically, and she tried to sit up, but his hands were on her wrists, firmly pressing them back on either side of her head, against the tapa-patterned cover.

"Don't move," he said. "I'm going." He stood up slowly, and his eyes ran down her body intimately, as though he knew every curve and line of it. She lay across the bed, her hair tangled, her cheeks flushed and eyes half-closed, the pathetic, inadequate armour of lipstick quite gone. "I want to hold that picture in my mind," he said softly, and bent to brush his lips across her cheek, before he left the room.

CHAPTER THIRTEEN

THEY flew home early on Saturday, losing a day in transit so that they arrived in Auckland on Sunday. Mark had left his car in the airport car park in readiness for the drive to Whangarei, and after a quick cup of coffee in the airport restaurant they were on their way north.

"You're quiet," Mark said. He had been driving for almost an hour, and although he had talked intermittently about the trip and the results of the meeting, Jacinth had scarcely managed more than a monosyllable or two in reply.

"I'm tired." It was the first excuse she thought of.

He cast her an unreadable glance and said, "Feel free to go to sleep, if you'd like."

Jacinth closed her eyes, to ward off further enquiry. She did feel tired, although she had slept surprisingly well last night, after Mark left her room. But as soon as she had wakened she had been assailed by an inexplicable anxiety that would not let her alone. Part of her was relieved and exultant that emotions she had once been convinced must have been left out of her nature had after all surfaced unmistakably. And part of her was bewildered and frankly terrified by the unexpected force of her feelings. Her undoubted emotional and physical reaction to Mark's lovemaking had shocked and amazed her. She had been totally unprepared for such unadulterated, almost frightening, depths of pleasure, and wasn't at all sure that in retrospect she liked the loss of control that it threatened. The thought of how she might react if

he ever made love to her properly was enough to make
her shake.

When he stopped the car at her house Mark got out
and carried her case up the steps for her.

Hecate came trotting around the side of the house,
mewing pathetically, as though she had been totally ne-
glected, and stalked into the house ahead of them,
straight through to the back door, where she stood waving her tail from side to side and complaining with increasing dudgeon until Jacinth opened that door, too.
She had asked Darrel to come and feed the cat each day,
but Hecate's behaviour made her wonder if he had for
some reason failed to do so—until she saw the uneaten
food still in the plate, and the milk in the saucer.

"You horrible animal!" she scolded. "A liar on top of
everything else. You're not even hungry!"

The cat wound itself around her legs, purring loudly,
and Mark came in. "I've put the case in your bedroom.
Looks as though Hecate is glad to see you."

"She's as contrary as—as—"

"As her mistress?" Mark suggested, a teasing smile on
his lips.

"I'm not contrary," Jacinth denied. "Anyway, I'm not
her mistress. You said cats are never owned."

Mark laughed. "So I did."

Hecate trotted out to the porch and began attacking
the cat food.

"I don't know why she didn't eat it before," Jacinth
said, changing the subject.

"Maybe she's been missing you."

Jacinth cast him a look of disbelief, and shut the door,
turning to find him much closer than she had expected.

"Would you like some coffee?" she asked him, saying the first thing that came into her head. "Or lunch?
It's actually well past lunchtime." She wished immediately that she hadn't issued an invitation, but it was too

late to retract it, and it did have the effect of making him step back, although he looked at her rather searchingly.

"If you can rustle something up," he said. "And this time I will help."

They ate in the kitchen, and she managed to keep up a smooth flow of innocuous conversation while she took sliced bread and a cheesecake from the freezer and opened tins of salmon and asparagus for sandwiches. Mark seemed content to follow her lead, but after they had finished eating and she got up from the table to make coffee, he reached out and caught her wrist in hard fingers.

"Jacinth! Skip the coffee. Tell me what's the matter."

All her automatic defences immediately came to the fore at the frontal attack. "Nothing," she said. "Are you sure you don't want coffee? It's no trouble."

His voice hardened. "Don't retreat from me again, Jacinth. We've come too far for that. The island sun melted the ice with a vengeance, and you can't just freeze over again. It won't work."

She looked down at the hand holding her wrist. "You're being rather silly, aren't you? A few kisses in the moonlight don't mean I'm yours to manhandle as you like."

He shot to his feet, his mouth tightening dangerously. She tried to pull away, but he retained his grip, and there was an angry little tussle, until she wrenched herself out of his hold and backed up against the counter, rubbing at the red mark on her wrist.

Mark took a visible check on himself as his eyes followed her movement. "Are you all right?" he asked abruptly.

Her lips barely moved. "Yes."

"I don't want to hurt you, Jacinth."

"You have a funny way of showing it."

He flushed. "I'm sorry. Will you tell me something?"

Warily, she said, "That depends on what it is, doesn't it?"

"Did Philip get more than 'a few kisses in the moonlight'?"

There was no reason why she should tell him, but she shrugged and said stonily, "No."

A strange expression flitted across his face, and she remembered telling Philip, "I didn't think anyone took that kind of thing seriously."

"What did you *think*?" she demanded.

Mark said, "I'm sure you know."

Her eyes were very green and coolly hostile. She turned abruptly and walked out of the kitchen, across the hall and into the lounge. She didn't know why, just that she had to get away from him, and the kitchen was very small.

Of course he followed her. She swung round in the middle of the room to stare at him, her hands thrust into the pockets of her skirt. "What else do you want to know?" she asked sarcastically.

And Mark, after a brief flash of surprise, said evenly, "Did he get the sort of response that I got last night?"

"Yes," she said briefly, after the barest hesitation, and turned away from him to walk over to the window.

He said softly, "I think you're lying, Jacinth."

"No—"

"*Yes*. Look at me."

She turned to face him, carefully controlled.

Mark trod softly towards her until he was within touching distance.

"I've learned to read you. Oh, you're awfully good at hiding what you feel, but little things give you away. Like this, for instance." He raised his hand and pressed a finger fleetingly against the hammering pulse at her temple. His finger trailed down to her cheek, almost as though he couldn't help taking a tactile pleasure in the feel of her skin. She flinched away. "And the way you turn your head a little and bring down your eyelids," Mark went on. "It looks like a supercilious gesture, but really it hides the look in your eyes. You use it when you're hurt, or sometimes when you're angry."

Inwardly trembling, she said, "You're imagining things."

"I'm not. I've watched you for a long time now. I'm beginning to understand what makes you tick. It's been— intriguing—finding out about you. That night on the beach was quite a revelation. I had begun to wonder if I'd been wrong about your response to me when I kissed you before. But there was no mistake on Rarotonga. That was genuine passion, there wasn't a doubt of it. You sent me away, but it wasn't easy, was it? I still remember how you looked when I left you."

His eyes recalled it to her, slipping down over her body, on his mouth a small curve of male possessiveness. "I've wondered, ever since I first saw you, if any woman could be that cold, a statue in ice," he said, "and now I know about the fire inside you. Because at last you became a living, breathing, *feeling* woman. *For me.*"

That night he had turned her world upside down, changed her view of herself forever. And she hadn't had time to adjust to that. He seemed to be claiming some kind of victory, a male triumph over a female who had challenged his virility. The idea chilled her, shamed her.

She said, shrugging away from his hands, "I suppose I'm not immune to the spell of the islands. Aren't tropical nights notorious for making people feel romantic— and it was all there, wasn't it? The whole cliché of swaying palms and coral sands and moonlight on the lagoon. I was even dressed for the part. We both got a bit carried away, but now we're back in the real world, and—"

"Stop it!"

His voice halted her, and she closed her mouth firmly, her expression totally wooden. His eyes glittered angrily, and he said, "I'm damned if I'm going to let you freeze me out again, Jacinth. We shared something *real* then. And don't you try to pretend it was just some sort of tropical dream, or temporary insanity!"

That seemed to describe it rather well, she thought. "It really wasn't more than that," she said. "For either of us. It would be best if we both forgot the whole thing, don't you think?"

"No I do not!" he said furiously. He reached for her with grim purpose. "Somehow I'm going to get through to you."

She whirled, trying to run from him, hitting out at him when he caught her wrist. Her hand glanced off his chin, and he grinned down at her derisively, and grabbed at that wrist, too, clipping them both behind her, his face full of deadly purpose.

"No!" she said, whipping her head aside to avoid his mouth.

He kissed her neck, his lips sliding threateningly up to the line of her jaw, and when she tried to kick him, he laughed and bent her backwards until she could barely stand. "Kiss me, Jacinth," he murmured, his lips against her cheek.

Fiercely, she said, "I hate you!"

"Well, at least it's an emotion." He released one wrist, still holding the other behind her, and his hand turned her head towards him. Her closed fist thudded against his shoulder, but he didn't even flinch. His eyes were on her mouth, and the intent look on his face suddenly terrified her. She remembered the mindless languor he had induced in her last night, remembered how vulnerable he could make her, without a will of her own, out of control and held in the grip of his masculine power to arouse her. She was suddenly trembling, and she saw his mouth

curve into a smile as his hold tightened on her, his head
bending to kiss her. Her fright transmuted into anger, and
she lifted her free hand a little farther, raking her nails
down the side of his face and neck.

His head jerked back, and she felt a small surge of
shockingly primitive satisfaction. But it was short-lived.
Her hand was suddenly jammed against him as he held
her suffocatingly close. "Been learning from your familiar, have you?" he asked with grim humour, and his
mouth found hers in a kiss that was full of angry frustration, desperate desire and a punitive determination to
force her submission.

He didn't stop until she went still and rigid in his arms.
When he did let her go, she stepped back with her eyes
blazing, her lips stinging and tender, and without even
thinking about it, she swung back her hand and hit him
hard.

He didn't try to avoid it, just stood there and took it as
if it was what he expected. She braced herself for retali-
ation, but he didn't move. Then the harsh, shrill sound
of the phone ringing broke the tension. Mark said,
"Leave it!" But she ignored that and brushed past him
into the hall.

"Jacinth!" her mother's voice said in her ear. "Thank
goodness you're home! I'm coming over, right now." She
sounded as though she was crying.

"What's the matter?" Jacinth asked.

"It's Lyle! He—oh, you won't believe this! I didn't
know he could be so—violent."

"Violent?" Jacinth said sharply. "How violent?"

Her mother sobbed, and said incoherently, "I'm
coming over, I can't stay here with him. I shouldn't have
married him."

Jacinth put the phone down slowly. Mark was standing in the doorway, his face oddly pale, except for four

narrow red weals on his cheek where she had scratched him.

She looked at him with returning hostility. "That was my mother. She said your father had been violent to her."

His brows went up in disbelief. "*Dad*? Rubbish!"

"My mother isn't a liar!"

"She's exaggerating," he said flatly. "He might have yelled a bit—when he blows up it can be impressive, though he doesn't get angry easily. But he would never hit a woman."

Stubbornly, Jacinth said, "She's very distressed."

"I have the impression," Mark said, "that Nadine is the type to get upset rather easily."

"She's highly strung."

"Is that what she told you?"

He looked disparaging, and Jacinth bristled defensively. "What are you implying?"

"Nothing." He seemed fed up, swinging away from her to return to the lounge, but then he changed his mind. "No," he said decisively, the glitter of anger still lurking in his eyes. "Maybe it's time you began to think about your mother, and the effect she's had on you."

"What on earth are you talking about?"

"You're frightened of emotion, aren't you, Jacinth?" he challenged. "Scared stiff that you might give yourself away, let other people know how you feel inside. The exact opposite of your mother, in fact. She's got rather a habit of telling all and sundry about her feelings. And really, hers are pretty shallow."

"That's not fair!" Jacinth said. "How dare you have the nerve to start analysing my mother!"

"It might throw some light on *your* hang-ups, if you'd think about it," he returned.

Jacinth curled her lip disdainfully. "That line has whiskers on it, Mark. I've lost count of the times a man has accused me of having sexual hang-ups because I didn't want to go to bed with him."

Mark simply ignored that. "Do you realise your mother is jealous of you?" he asked.

Jacinth blinked. *"Jealous?"*

"Why else does she put you down so consistently?"

Jacinth gasped. "You're crazy! Actually she has an embarrassing habit of praising me. You must have noticed, at the dinner party—"

"I noticed," Mark cut in flatly. "Everything she said hid an implied 'but'. And she always managed to compare herself with you, pretending to admire you, to be proud of you, but in reality *she* was the one who was supposedly more feminine, more attractive, more sweet and self-sacrificing."

"Oh, nonsense! You're twisting things . . ."

"Do you know what I think?" he went on remorselessly. "I think it's been going on for years—probably from the time you first began to grow into a woman, and she realised that her own youth was slipping away. Nadine is one of those ultrafeminine women whose self-image is built around the notion of sex appeal. A beautiful daughter was a rival, and she had to defend her position. She's managed to sap your confidence in yourself, in your personality, your capacity to love, to have people love you—or even like you. And you've hidden yourself away in a hard little shell so that no one can know you, and you can't be hurt. You have no trust in people—certainly not in men."

"If I don't trust men," Jacinth said, "it's because I've seen what they've done to my mother."

Exasperated, he said, "She isn't the only deserted woman in the world, Jacinth! Your father may have let her down—"

"It wasn't only my father! It was every man she's ever had a relationship with! Including *your* father, apparently!"

Mark said slowly, his eyes suddenly intent, "How many relationships would that be?"

Jacinth flushed angrily. "If you're implying that she was promiscuous—"

"I'm not implying anything of the sort."

"It certainly sounded like it! You talk about jealousy—I think you're the one who's jealous, Mark. Jealous of my mother, because of her place in your father's life. Because she's taken your mother's place."

Mark opened his mouth; then he hesitated, seeming to actually consider the idea. "No," he said finally. "That's not true. I had doubts, because Nadine was so different from my own mother. I didn't know if she could make my father happy. Because he and my mother were very happy, Jacinth. I do remember that."

"My mother is as good as—"

Mark suddenly gave a crack of laughter. "Let's not start this," he said. "We're beginning to sound like a couple of kids in a school playground. My father's marriage is his own business, and I've no intention of interfering. *You'd* be wise to let them sort out their own marital problems, too. Nadine wants to cry on your shoulder, I gather."

"I don't need your advice, thank you!"

"OK." He shrugged. "I'm sorry if I've put forward some unpalatable truths—"

"Theories!" Jacinth snapped.

"All right, theories. But the only reason I'm interested in Nadine's—foibles—is because of their effect on you. You're the one that I care about, Jacinth."

Coldly, she said, "You don't *care* about me, Mark. At least, only in the way a biologist cares about a butterfly he's about to impale on a pin."

His eyes narrowed. "What are you talking about?"

"Some men have an irresistible urge to 'conquer' a woman who doesn't want them."

Mark said, angrily, "I'm not one of them, Jacinth!"

"You find me interesting as a kind of psychological puzzle, but mainly as a sexual challenge. You wanted to melt the ice-maiden. You said so."

"All right, I said so," he admitted. His voice was clipped in the extreme.

"Well, helped by a bit of tropical moonlight, you succeeded, temporarily," she said lightly. "So chalk it up. Congratulations. But it won't happen again."

"*Jacinth—*" He leaned toward her, his hands reaching for her.

"And please don't try mauling me again," she said icily. "Maybe it gives you some kind of perverted satisfaction to impose your kisses on a woman by brute force, but next time, I'll charge you with assault."

He straightened, his face darkening.

Jacinth turned her back on him and went into the living room. When he joined her she wouldn't look at him, hoping he would take the hint and leave, and they waited in tense silence.

Then quick footsteps sounded outside.

"Your mother," Mark said, sardonically.

"You'll have to go!" Jacinth said, darting to open the door.

Mark folded his arms, leaning against the jamb of the lounge door. "I think I'll stay," he said, his careless pose not disguising the fact that he was deeply furious. "This promises to be rather enlightening."

CHAPTER FOURTEEN

NADINE flew inside on a cloud of perfume and an ocean of tears, and cast herself dramatically on Jacinth's shoulder, sobbing brokenheartedly.

At first she didn't even see Mark, who hadn't responded to Jacinth's pointed glare, but did look slightly discomfited when Nadine raised her head and said tragically, "Mark! Oh, I didn't want *you* to see me like this!" and then buried her face in her hands.

Jacinth thought he probably hadn't bargained on the tears. She took her mother into the lounge, saying acidly to Mark as he stood aside, "Well if you're going to stay, you might as well be useful. Will you pour a glass of sherry for her, please."

He complied, bringing the glass to Nadine on the sofa, where Jacinth had her arm about her mother.

Nadine drank some, and mopped her eyes with an embroidered handkerchief. "I'm sorry," she said mournfully. "You must think I'm very silly."

"That depends on what it's all about," Mark said.

"Oh," she said, sniffing, "I expect you'll say it's nothing."

Mark glanced at Jacinth. He said evenly, "You gave Jacinth the impression that my father had beaten you, or at least threatened to."

"Well..." She wiped her eyes, peeked at him from behind the handkerchief, then looked away.

"He didn't, did he?" Mark asked.

Jacinth said, "Mark—"

"Did he?" Mark insisted quietly.

"Not exactly," Nadine admitted. "But he was so angry—" She said defiantly, "I was frightened!"

Mark grinned faintly. "Well, he scared me a couple of times when I was a kid. But not without reason, and it soon blows over, you know."

"He had no right to shout at me," she said sulkily. "And all over a couple of silly old pictures. They're not even very good! Just because *Margot* painted them—"

"My mother's flower paintings?" Mark said sharply.

"Your mother painted?" Jacinth asked. She hadn't known that. But she hadn't even known his mother's name. Everyone had avoided mentioning Lyle's first wife, in deference to Nadine's feelings.

"She was quite a good painter," Mark explained curtly, his eyes on Nadine. "She only did it for her own pleasure. Most of her paintings were given away to friends and family. But a couple of flower studies were hung in the hall at home."

"I remember," Jacinth said. She had rather liked them, although flower studies were not her favourite form of art. "What happened?" she asked Nadine.

"Well, Lyle *told* me I could do what I liked with the house," Nadine said resentfully. "Before the wedding, he even offered to sell it and buy something else, if I didn't want to live in a place he'd shared with *her*. But I like the house, it's just the sort of place I always wanted, and I thought, I'll make it mine. And he said he understood my wanting to have my own things, instead of hers. So I got rid of the paintings—"

"Got rid of...?" Mark said, stiffening. *"How?"*

"I burnt them," Nadine said defiantly. "At least, I tried to. But he saw me putting them in the incinerator, and shouted at me.... He pulled them out. I think he got burnt, too—"

"He's *hurt*?" Mark exclaimed. Jacinth glanced at him, and saw that he had gone very white, the skin taut on his face.

"Oh, not badly, I'm sure. It was too quick for that. And then he swore at me, terribly, and—I ran into the house and phoned Jacinth. Well, he *was* frightening, and if he still loves Margot more than me, he shouldn't have asked me to marry him!"

She began sobbing again, and Mark gave Jacinth a stunned, furious look, then said to Nadine rather tightly, "Didn't it occur to you that if you couldn't bear having them about the house, Darrel or I might have been glad to have them?"

Her voice muffled in the handkerchief, she said, "I didn't think.... I just couldn't bear looking at them any longer."

Mark's jaw clenched. Jacinth felt sick, and appalled.

The telephone rang, and Jacinth went to answer it.

It was Lyle, asking if Nadine was there. "She can't come to the phone," Jacinth told him. "She's—rather agitated."

He said, "We both were. I'm coming round."

Jacinth said doubtfully, "Perhaps you should wait awhile—"

He paused for a moment. "I don't think so."

She went back to her mother and Mark. "Lyle's coming over."

Nadine looked up, horrified. "Oh, no! I must look a fright! Jacinth—my make-up—the bathroom."

She fled in haste, and Mark started to laugh, rather harshly.

"It's not funny!" Jacinth flashed. "She's very upset."

When Lyle arrived, with one hand roughly bandaged, Nadine was sitting on the sofa, prettily made-up and sipping a cup of tea that Jacinth had made for her. She looked up apprehensively, then exclaimed, "Oh, Lyle! Your poor hand! Is it bad?"

He shook his head. "It's just a surface burn—a bit sore, that's all."

Mark, who had opened the door, glanced meaningfully at Jacinth and said, "We'll leave you two alone."

Nadine looked vaguely alarmed. "Don't go...." she said, clutching at her daughter's arm.

Lyle sat down at her other side and took her hand in his unbandaged one. "Don't be silly, Nadine, I'm not going to hurt you. I love you."

Nadine looked doubtful, tears trembling again on her lashes. "But—you frightened me, shouting and swearing like that...."

Lyle lifted her hand in his and kissed it. "I'm sorry I yelled at you, sweetheart. I got a bit of a shock. I understand that you didn't want the paintings, but we could have given them to someone."

"I just don't want to be reminded of her," Nadine said pitifully. "I don't mean to be jealous and horrid, but I can't help it. I want you to love *me*."

Mark was leaning against the door frame, his arms folded and a fascinated expression on his face. Jacinth eased gently away from her mother's slackening hold on her arm.

"Of *course* I love you," Lyle said. "I love you very much." He looked at Nadine thoughtfully, then seemed to make a resolution. Firmly, he added, "But I can't pretend that Margot never existed, you know. You don't have to live with her things, but I won't let you destroy them. For one thing, it wouldn't be fair to my boys."

Nadine's face went sulky, her eyes misty with tears, and her lips pouting. "You still love her, don't you? Was she prettier than me?"

Lyle frowned. Jacinth cast a swift glance at Mark, to see that his expression had gone shuttered.

Lyle's face cleared, and Jacinth thought a fleeting look of compassion came into his eyes. Smiling a little, he said gently, "No, Margot wasn't prettier than you. And I still *remember* the love I had for her. But I *love you*, Nadine. Until death do us part."

"Oh," she breathed, gazing into his face. "Oh, Lyle!" She threw herself on his chest, sobbing, and as he closed his arms about her, Jacinth stood up and said to Lyle, "Would you like a cup of tea?"

"Thank you, Jacinth," he said.

Mark followed her out of the room. "Well, that seems to be a satisfactory conclusion," he said on a decidedly cynical note. "Lesson one on how to handle a hysterical woman."

"She wasn't hysterical," Jacinth snapped, going into the kitchen. "She was hurt."

"*She* was? My father was pretty hurt, too."

"It wasn't her fault he got burnt. She didn't know he was even around."

"That isn't what I meant, and I think you know it. I don't envy my father."

Jacinth turned on him. "That's a beastly thing to say! He loves her!"

"I suppose he does. But at least he's not so besotted that he'll allow her to get away with emotional black-mail."

"She wouldn't do that!"

"Oh, *come on*!" He checked himself, and appeared to think better of what he was going to say.

"What did you mean by that?" Jacinth demanded. "You've gone so far, you might as well tell me what you're getting at."

"I think you know perfectly well what I meant. She's been doing it to you for years, hasn't she?"

"You *are* jealous!" Jacinth said acidly. "What on earth will you come up with next? I never heard anything so crazy."

"Oh, the hell with it!" he said irritably, flinging out a hand. "What's the use! I've said enough, anyway."

Coldly furious, she said, "Yes, I think you have. Do you think your presence is really required here any more?"

"You want me to go?"

"Yes." She wouldn't forgive him for what he had said about her mother; it had been cruel and unfair, and she resented his assessment of Nadine's relationship with her.

"I admire your loyalty, Jacinth. But you can still love someone while acknowledging that they're not perfect, you know."

"Is there a charge for your pearls of wisdom?" she asked sarcastically. "Or do you dish them out free?"

"When you stop being angry with me," he suggested, "I wish you'd think about some of what I've been saying."

"You can see yourself out, can't you?" Pointedly, she turned away from him, and busied herself getting the tea.

"All right, little cat, I'll go. I'll see you tomorrow, at work."

Half an hour later, a rather subdued Nadine got ready to leave with her husband. Lyle came into the kitchen with the empty cups and said, "She's repairing her make-up. Your mother's a very insecure person, isn't she? I'm afraid I didn't realise that. I never expected her to be so— so sensitive about being a second wife. I can't pretend that I didn't love Margot, you know," he added, looking troubled. "It wouldn't be right."

"Of course not. No one expects you to," Jacinth agreed.

"Nadine did. She thought that rescuing Margot's pictures and getting burnt in the process was a sure sign that my first wife meant more to me than *she* does. I should have taken down the pictures earlier, but they'd always been there, and I didn't really notice them any more. But it was wrong of her to burn them, Jacinth.''

"She's had some bad experiences with men she's grown fond of," Jacinth said hesitantly. "I think she needs to be very sure that she's loved."

"Yes, I'm beginning to realise that. She's different from Margot—for one thing, when I yelled at Margot, she yelled right back. Not that we fought often. But I didn't expect Nadine to go to pieces because of a few words spoken in temper. Mind you," he looked down at his bandaged hand, "part of it was because my hand was smarting somewhat after the rescue act."

"Is it really all right?" Jacinth said. "Should you have it looked at?"

"It's OK." He winked. "I'll get your mother to tend to it later. She's quite concerned."

"Were the pictures badly damaged?" Jacinth asked him, her voice low.

"No, the frames will have to be replaced, but the pictures themselves were only slightly scorched at the edges. I'm sure they'll be as good as new. I'll get them re-framed and give one each to Mark and Darrel."

Relieved, Jacinth said, "Oh, I'm glad about that." She wondered if he would have been so forgiving if Nadine had managed to carry out her intention of burning them. She wasn't sure if Mark would ever forgive her mother. "Mark was—very angry," she said.

"He's inherited my temper, I'm afraid." Lyle looked at her shrewdly. "Has he upset you?"

Jacinth shook her head. "It's been rather upsetting for all of us."

"Yes, and you just back from your trip. Well, your mother and I will leave you in peace soon."

After they had left, Jacinth found her knees were shaking, and realised that she was deathly tired. She sank onto her bed and slept for hours, only waking when something shook the mattress. It was dusk, and Hecate had found her and jumped up on the bed. Jacinth, lying on her side with her legs slightly bent, didn't move, and the cat sniffed at her face, turned round a couple of times, and snuggled up into the curve of her body.

"Hello, cat," Jacinth murmured.

Hecate twitched an ear, opened an eye. Cautiously, Jacinth put a hand on her head, and tentatively began to stroke her. Hecate wound her tail tightly about herself and started to purr.

Jacinth was reluctant to go to work on Monday. She dreaded seeing Mark, and there was still a hard lump of anger and resentment inside her when she thought of him.

"How's your mother?" Mark asked her politely. "Fireworks over?"

"As far as I know, she's all right," Jacinth answered composedly. She was relieved to see that his face was unmarked, the surface scratches she had inflicted quite gone.

He leaned back in his chair. "But you're still furious with me?"

"Not at all," she said. "You'll want a report on the island trip, won't you? I have my notes here."

His eyes narrowed, he looked at her steadily. Then he said brusquely, "All right, if that's the way you want it. There comes a time when beating one's head against a brick wall begins to look like deliberate masochism. And frankly, I've never gone in for that."

From then on, he treated her like a stranger. Even the careful friendliness of their former working relationship had disappeared. Mark only spoke to her when it was absolutely necessary, and any moment she expected him to start addressing her as "Miss Norwood." He was scrupulously polite, but when she made a mistake with some figures, he tore a strip off her in no uncertain terms.

Stiffly, her cheeks pale with humiliation and rage, Jacinth offered to resign, but he only stared at her coldly and said, "You promised me a year. You'll just have to stick it out."

"I only thought that if you're so dissatisfied with my work, you might prefer to appoint someone else."

"Don't be so touchy," he said irritably. "I merely pointed out that your figures are wrong. It could happen to anyone."

"Then why make an issue of it?" she demanded, adding, "And it's never happened to me before."

"Really?" He gave her a searching look. She made her face a blank, refusing to allow him to read her as he had once claimed he could. Before, it had been an automatic response to any strong feeling—her own or other people's. Now she had to consciously adopt the mask that hid pain and bewilderment. Somehow Mark had inflicted a permanent hole in her customary defences. And she was grimly determined not to let him know that the defeat he had conceded was for her a very hollow victory.

Mark was out a good deal now, overseeing arrangements for the first craft shop to be opened, in Whangarei. If that was a success, after six months the company hoped to start another in the larger city of Auckland. He went north again to check the schooner, which was nearing completion, but this time Jacinth wasn't invited.

While he was away, she took the opportunity to visit her mother and Lyle. Nadine had often pressed her to come and see them, but she didn't want to be there at the same time as Mark. It was bad enough having to brace

herself to see him every day, and have him look at her
with indifference. She didn't want to meet him outside
working hours.

Her mother seemed more content, less brittle. There
was a softness about her that Jacinth had never seen before, and her smiles were real and radiant. She confided
to Jacinth that she had been convinced, seeing Lyle brave
the flames to rescue his first wife's paintings, that Margot
would always be more important to him. "That's why I
ran away, really," she said. "Because I couldn't bear the
thought that I was second-best. But when he came
straight after me, even with his poor, burnt hand, I
thought, perhaps he does care for me, after all. And,"
she added, as her lashes fluttered shyly, "he convinced
me, in the end, that I mean just as much to him. And I
do, Jacinth. I really believe that man worships the ground
I walk on."

She sounded a trifle smug, but at least someone was
happy, Jacinth thought bleakly. Lyle might be madly in
love with Nadine, but he was no doormat, and she had an
idea that was the kind of man Nadine needed. What
Mark had said was true. Her mother had always made
her feel both guilty and inadequate, because unconsciously Nadine had tried to use her daughter to replace
the one thing she really wanted—a man in her life to love
and cherish her. Now that she had that, Jacinth realised,
Nadine no longer needed her so desperately.

For the first time in her life Jacinth was free of a bur-
den she hadn't realised she was carrying. It was a strange
feeling, of both lightness and emptiness.

Darrel turned up on the same afternoon, seemingly
blissfully unaware that there had been any crisis, and
showing an envious interest in Jacinth's impressions of
Rarotonga.

"You didn't have time to visit any of the outer islands?" he asked. "If you ever get the chance, Jacinth—

I spent part of my holiday on a boat, poking about them. The unspoiled Pacific.''

"We were only there for a few days," she reminded him. "On business.''

"Shame," Darrel said. "Tell Mark next time he'd better show you round properly, take a couple of extra days. Tell you what," he said, edging closer. "If I'd been alone with you on a Pacific island, I'd have made the most of the moonlight and the palm trees.''

With an effort, Jacinth managed to laugh. "I would have cramped your style," she said. "I'm sure you'd find a Polynesian beauty much more interesting.''

"Well, they are fantastic," he conceded. "Did you see the girls doing a *tamure* while you were there?" His eyes lit up rapturously. "Wow!''

"Yes," she said. "I even learned how to do it.''

"You did! Show me!''

Jacinth laughed, genuinely this time. "No. There's a time and place, but this isn't it.''

He had brought back memories, though. She went home with a huge, aching lump in her throat. Hecate greeted her at the door with demands for food, and after she had fed the cat and made a snack for herself, she sat at the table with her chin on her hands, thinking of warm nights and the insistent beat of a wooden drum, and kisses in the moonlight.

CHAPTER FIFTEEN

THE schooner was due to be launched about the time that the shop opened, so it was decided to combine the two events by having the launching with all due ceremony, on a Sunday, sailing the schooner down to Whangarei for the opening of the shop the next day.

"Tu and Tiari are flying over," Mark told Jacinth. "We should get a good crowd to the launching. There'll be a display of island crafts and goods there, and we'll encourage people to dress in island costume, and have a troupe of dancers performing. You must wear the *pareu* that Tiari gave you. They're looking forward to seeing you."

"It's a bit cool for that," she objected. Winter was passing, but she was still wearing a light jacket most days.

"I've ordered a couple of nice sunny days," he assured her with a narrow grin.

He'd probably get them, too, she thought. And she was right.

Mark invited his family to attend the launching, and Jacinth made an excuse to travel north with Lyle, Nadine and Darrel, instead of accepting Mark's suggestion that she should go with him. He took her refusal without protest, apparently not caring, and she despised herself for being hurt by his indifference. He was taking Tu and Tiari along; they had arrived the night before, and were using Mark's spare bedroom.

The sun was bright but had not attained its full summer warmth, and Jacinth compromised by wearing the *pareu* about her waist, and donning a cotton blouse with rolled sleeves, which she tied in a knot under her breasts, leaving her midriff bare. Nadine looked askance at her when she got into the car. She herself was wearing an elegant summer frock, and Lyle had on a sport shirt and trousers, but Darrel had opted for a brown and yellow print shirt, and when they were offered flowers from a basket held by a Polynesian girl in a hula skirt who greeted them at the wharf, he took one and stuck it behind his ear, and then did the same for Jacinth.

The two brothers, Ted and Oscar, who had built the schooner, vied with each other for the most brilliantly coloured shirt, Ted in shades of orange and blue, and Oscar in bright green with a pattern of scarlet hibiscus.

Tiari gave Jacinth a pleased smile and kissed her cheek, greeting her with, "*Kia orana*. Tu and Mark are busy with some last-minute arrangements. I've found us a good place to sit, over there." Tiari was wearing a pretty red and white *pareu*, and had flung across her shoulders like a shawl the very large tie-dyed silk scarf that Jacinth had sent to her as a gift. "It's lovely," Tiari said, fingering the silk as she saw Jacinth looking at it. "Thank you again, Jacinth."

There were woven mats scattered about on the wharf, a few folding chairs and various coils of rope, boxes and stacks of timber that people were utilising as makeshift seating. Lyle procured a chair for Nadine, and the rest of them sat on a pale woven mat with a criss-cross border.

The proceedings began with a dance display, which was hugely enjoyed by the crowd that had gathered to wish the schooner well on her maiden voyage. About halfway through, Jacinth was suddenly conscious that Mark had joined them and was sitting at her shoulder. After that she lost her absorption in the dancing. It was months since she had been this close to him, so close that as he moved to applaud a dance, she could feel the brush of his cotton shirt against her shoulder; and if she turned her

head a little she could see the hard outline of his chin, and
feel his breath stirring tendrils of hair on her forehead.
When the display finished with a rousing rendition of the
tamure, he leaned closer, his shoulder pressing lightly
against hers. She kept her eyes rigidly to the front. He put
his arm lightly about her shoulders, but as the dance
ended, his fingers gripped and held for a second or two
before he moved to applaud the end of the show.

He got up then and went to compère the formal
launching ceremony.

Jacinth hardly noticed the island dignitaries who per-
formed the solemn part of the launching in accordance
with their own custom, or the local celebrity who had
been asked to crack the bottle of champagne over the
hull. She watched Mark with an intensity that she
thought he must have felt, unable to take her eyes off his
tall, lithe figure, watching the way the breeze ruffled his
dark hair, the way he bent to listen to a brown-skinned
child who tugged at his hand, his easy smile, his quiet
confidence, and the pleasure in his face as the schooner
finally slid smoothly into the water.

The crowd cheered, and the drumbeat began again
while several dancers standing at the edge of the wharf
broke into an apparently spontaneous *tamure*. Amid
laughter and clapping, old and young people joined in,
and the Polynesians teasingly began drawing people from
the crowd to partner them. Several young men joined in
with zest, and teenage girls, blushing and giggling, tried
to match the expert hip-swinging of the island women.

Tu, smiling broadly, swooped on Jacinth and drew her,
protesting, to her feet, but it would have been bad man-
nered and churlish to turn him down, and recklessly she
kicked off her shoes and began to recall the sensual,
rhythmic movements Tiari had taught her. Tiari was
dancing with Darrel, who was obviously enjoying himself hugely, and then Mark had interposed himself be-

tween Jacinth and Tu, challenging her in the island way
by sidling up, keeping time with the drumbeat, his hands
over his head as he grinned down at her. Tu laughed at
him, shrugged at Jacinth, and went off to find another
partner.

She looked into Mark's gleaming eyes and smiled back
at him. The drumbeat went on and on, there was noise
and colour and movement all around, the wharf vibrat-
ing under the dancers' feet. Jacinth tossed her hair back
and danced, intoxicated by the primitive music, the
rhythm, the unmistakable message that she read in
Mark's eyes.

Her cheeks were flushed with the energetic movements of the dance. When the music finally stopped, she
was panting, her eyes shining. She put a hand to her hair,
drawing it back off her shoulders, and the flower behind
her ear fell to the ground. Mark swooped and picked it
up, and tucked it behind his own ear. "I have to talk to
some people," he said. "See you later." And abruptly he
wheeled and was gone.

The crowd was breaking up, and Tiari and Tu had
wandered off. Jacinth went back to Nadine and Lyle, and
her mother looked at her curiously. "I didn't know you
could do that," she said, as though she wasn't sure she
approved.

"I learned it in Rarotonga," Jacinth said. "It's fun."

Nadine smiled doubtfully, a little bemused. "I suppose it is," she said. "You obviously enjoyed it."

Jacinth felt a light tug at her arm, and turned to see
Philip Rotch at her side, tentatively smiling.

"Jacinth," he said. "I haven't seen you for ages." That
wasn't quite true. She had seen him several times in
Whangarei; it wasn't a very big town. But he had plainly
not wanted to spend time talking to her, so she had
passed him with a nod and a smile, usually receiving the
same in return.

"Hello, Philip," she said. "You're looking well."

"You too," he said. "I like your hair down, it suits you." He nodded to Nadine over her shoulder, then looked back at her. "I saw you dancing. You were terrific."

"Thank you."

Darrel touched her shoulder. "See you at the car." Nadine and Lyle were moving away ahead of him.

Jacinth said, "I won't be long." But she couldn't just cut Philip off, the first time he had felt able to speak to her since she had left the firm.

"New boyfriend?" Philip asked.

Jacinth shook her head. "No." She explained about her mother's second marriage, and Philip said, "That'll be good for her. For you, too, I dare say. She always tended to smother you a bit, I thought."

"Did you?" Jacinth said coolly.

"Sorry if I'm treading on the grass," he said. "I'm sure it was understandable, but it can't have been good for either of you. Anyway," he looked her over with admiration and a certain wistfulness, "it looks as though you're breaking out a bit."

"This is a special occasion," she said. "I don't always dress like this."

He laughed, quite easily. "I know that. There is something different about you, though, Jacinth. Maybe it's because you've let your hair down—literally. Somehow you seem more—vulnerable."

She smiled, shaking her head. "I'm sure you're imagining things."

"Am I?" he queried. "Maybe."

A few moments later he was about to move off when she said, "Philip?"

"Yes?"

"Are you all right? I mean . . ."

"Am I getting over you?" he said bluntly. "Yes, I guess so. I don't spend every waking moment thinking of you any more. I don't want to burst into tears every time I see you on the street. There—isn't a chance you'd change your mind, I suppose?"

Jacinth shook her head. "I'm sorry, Philip."

"I didn't think so. I used to wish you knew what it was like, that you could be as miserable as I was. Now, I just want you to be happy, Jacinth. Take care."

"Yes," she said. "You too, Philip."

She gave him her hand, and he smiled crookedly and bent to brush her cheek with his lips. When he had gone, she stood gazing abstractedly at the *Kia Orana*, with a leaden lump where her heart should have been.

I know what it's like, she thought bleakly. Because she had learned, in the past few months, how it felt to be in daily contact with someone without whom her life would become dry and empty, knowing that he didn't feel at all the same way about her.

She turned to see Mark coming towards her, and in spite of herself, her spirits lifted, because just watching him gave her such pleasure. Involuntarily, she smiled gladly, and thought that his eyes held a warmth that had been missing lately.

"I'm taking you back with me," he said. "I saw Lyle and the others in the car park, and told them to go on home."

When they were in the car, she said, "What about Tu and Tiari?"

"They're sailing down in the schooner. Didn't you know?"

She knew some people were going along on the short voyage; there had been a suggestion that Mark might join them, but he had decided to stay on land in case there was any hitch between the launching and the gala opening of the shop tomorrow.

"Have a good time?" he asked her as they drove away.

"Yes. It was a very successful launch, Mark. Congratulations."

"Thank you. That was Philip you were talking to, wasn't it?"

"Yes." Something in his voice made her tense a little.

"You looked rather pensive, after he left you. Are you regretting turning him down?"

"No," she said. "Only regretting that I hurt him."

He cast a glance at her, and went on driving in silence. She wanted to say something, explain that she hadn't been deliberately cold-blooded, that she wasn't unfeeling. But she was afraid of saying the wrong thing, of wrecking what seemed to be a tentative groping towards a new stage in their relationship.

When they came to the bluff where they had climbed to the lookout before, he stopped the car quite suddenly, as though he had intended to pass by and changed his mind.

Jacinth felt her heart begin to pick up a quicker beat, and without looking at her he said, "Would you like to climb up and look at the view again?"

She swallowed, suddenly frightened. "Don't you have to get back?"

"We have time," he said, and turned to look at her. His expression seemed rather hostile. "Nobody's forcing you. Yes or no?"

"Yes," she said quickly, recklessly. She couldn't meet his eyes as she got out of the car, but when he took her hand while they were climbing the path, she looked up and saw him smiling down at her, his eyes brilliant and probing, and she stopped for a moment, breathless, until his hand tugged her forward and suddenly into his arms.

She drowned in his kiss, her lips softly parted, his hand on her bare midriff, the other holding hers tightly. Then he put her away from him, and in total silence resumed the climb.

At the top, they stood side by side, looking out over the sunlight on the sea, and Mark pointed to a white sailing ship making proudly for the horizon outside the bay and said huskily, "There she is."

They watched in silence, their linked fingers entwined, until she was out of sight. No one came to disturb them, and at last Mark turned to her and said softly, "Have you forgiven me yet?"

She raised her eyes to his. "A long time ago. But I didn't think you were—interested."

It seemed that he had easily shrugged off whatever hold she might have had on his emotions. He hadn't been in very deep, and had turned back before whatever he had felt—curiosity, desire—had time to turn into love, if there had ever been that possibility. But he had left her floundering, in over her head, hopelessly out of her depth. Hopelessly in love.

"If you'd given me the slightest sign . . ." he said.

"I thought you could read me like a book."

"I knew you weren't happy. But I also thought you were still hating me."

Jacinth said, her eyes sweeping down, "I never hated you, Mark."

"So—" he drawled, his own eyes relentless on her down-bent head, "tell me how you feel about me, Jacinth."

That frightened her again, and beneath the fear there was a stirring of anger. "That's not fair," she said, and tried to tug her hand from his hold. She still wasn't sure what he wanted, expected, of her. She had accused him of trying to melt the ice-maiden, and he hadn't denied it. Maybe that was all it was to him; he wanted her unconditional surrender, without committing himself at all.

Was it merely to build up his own ego? To prove his theories about her?

Instinct told her that Mark wasn't like that, that he wasn't the sort of man who would play with her emotions for some selfish, shallow reason. But still she was afraid to trust her instinct, afraid of letting him know her feelings in case he couldn't share them.

He closed his fingers firmly over hers and with his other hand made her face him. "Why can't you tell me?" And she saw that he knew, that he was teasing, a gleam of humour in his eyes, and supreme male confidence, and then he bent and kissed her mouth with a tenderness that had the effect of throwing her into a turmoil.

She wrenched herself away from him, saying wildly, "Why can't *you* tell *me*?" And when he reached for her she struck his hand away blindly, saying with fierce resentment, "*No!* Don't touch me! You don't love me, you're trying to prove something to yourself, or me—I don't know! I can't—I won't let you reduce me to a bundle of quivering emotion, hanging on your every word and saying 'I love you' on cue like some Pavlov's dog! You can't make me into some sort of talking, walking doll, dependent on you for my happiness, for my very existence, only half-alive because you're not smiling at me! I'll get over it. I *don't need you*. You have no *right* to make me feel like this. I can manage without you in my life."

Mark, who had been looking at her with blank surprise, suddenly began laughing, and a hot, bursting tide of rage welled up inside her and spilled over. "And don't you laugh at me!" she shouted, and launched herself at him, her fists beating his hard chest, until he grabbed her wrists, still laughing, and held her. Enraged, she struggled against him, her face flushed and her eyes glittering with angry tears. And he stopped laughing, but wouldn't let her go.

She freed one hand, but he captured it again as she lifted it in the air, and caught her against him, holding her tightly, and started talking to her, his voice low and urgent. "Darling, don't. There's no need."

"Let me *go*!" she sobbed through gritted teeth.

"No!" His grip tightened, and she felt his lips on her temple, her averted cheek, her eyelid. "Don't," he murmured. "It's all right, I love you, Jacinth. *I love you.* I thought you knew that."

She moved disbelievingly, trying to break his hold, but he wouldn't let go. "Listen to me," he said softly. "Please, Jacinth. I love you. I don't want to let you go, ever. Do you hear that? Not ever."

He was still kissing her—warm, urgent, almost desperate little kisses all over her face, her neck, wherever he could reach. "Jacinth, love," he whispered. "Love, please. I wasn't trying to torture you, or humble you. It wasn't a power play. I just needed to hear you say it. Because you might be able to manage without me, but I sure as hell don't fancy trying to live without you."

Gradually she stopped resisting him, beginning to respond to the insistent tenderness in his voice. Her body relaxed against him, and she turned her head and looked into his eyes, questioning, almost daring to believe him, and finally accepting that he meant what he was telling her over and over.

"Jacinth?" he said at last, and smoothed her hair back from her face with gentle hands.

"I love you," she said, and at the sudden blaze in his eyes, she locked her arms about his neck and lifted her mouth eagerly to his.

The world rocked, the only beings in it this man and this woman, her mouth under his, his hands caressing the skin of her back, touching her hair, her face, her body that softly curved to the hard warmth of his.

They parted reluctantly, and Mark's hands moved on her bare midriff, sliding from back to front and then to her back again, where his fingers began exploring her spine. Her hands were on his arms, and her eyes were shining. He put his hand up to her hair again, stroking it, and she looked up at him, and said, "You've lost your flower."

It was crushed on the ground at their feet. Mark picked it up and said, "It fell off when you attacked me."

Jacinth said, "I don't know what came over me."

He tucked the ruined flower carefully into his shirt pocket and said, "Anger. A good, strong, healthy emotion. For once you let it all out, and it was a sight to see."

"I've never done anything like that before in my life."

"Is it so scary, being in love with me?" he asked her quietly.

She thought. "Yes," she said. "When I thought you didn't love me."

Mark shook his head. "I don't know how you could have believed that. I thought that in Rarotonga, you knew I was head over heels in love with you, that I was just biding my time, waiting for you to admit that you loved me, too."

"But—you said you were sick of beating your head against a brick wall. I thought you were washing your hands of me."

"You think I *could*? You're in my heart, in my head, in my mind. You're my soul, Jacinth. I might have said what I did in any case, but by criticising your mother when I was in a flaming, white-hot rage, I knew I'd committed a major tactical error. From then on, all I could do was patiently wait for you to come round, and hope that propinquity would help."

"Propinquity just about drove me crazy," Jacinth admitted.

"Well, good. Because at times it was all I could do to stop myself from dragging you out of your chair and making love to you there and then."

"Sometimes I wished you would."

"I thought I'd get my eyes scratched out."

"Well—I suppose I might have done that. It took me a long time to admit to myself how I really felt. And that . . . you were right about some things."

He grinned affectionately down at her. "No wonder I was scared to touch you."

"You weren't scared." She scoffed. "You were just playing a waiting game, like you did with Hecate."

He put his arm about her and began walking her towards the path that led to the road. "How is Hecate?"

"Getting fat. She'll be furious with me when we get home, by the way. We're late. I'll be treated to cold stares all night."

"I sympathise. I've been treated to cold stares all winter. We'll buy her a nice fresh fish to compensate. Couldn't you find her a home, after all?"

Jacinth said firmly, "She's got a home. Anyway, who would have had her?"

He laughed. "How do you fancy a honeymoon cruise on a schooner going to the islands?"

"On the *Kia Orana*?" She turned to him, her eyes alight. "I'd love it, of course."

"Then you'll have to marry me soon."

"I don't mind. What will we do with Hecate, though? I can't ask Darrel to feed her for more than a few days."

"Maybe she could live with Dad and your mother for a while. They've a big enough property."

"My mother would never have her."

"Oh, I don't know. Hecate might cast a spell on her, and have Nadine eating out of her hand."

"The other way round, surely," Jacinth said. "Or is it?"

"Does she eat out of *your* hand, yet?"

"She eats off a plate and snarls at me if I come near. She does sleep with me sometimes, though."

His brows rose. "Does she indeed? Well, you had better explain to her that you're going to have another bed partner in the near future."

"*You* explain to her," Jacinth suggested. "You're so good with cats."

"I'll bribe her with a nice basket from the trade shop," he said. "She can sleep in that."

"You can try."

"I brought *you* round, darling. Compared with that, Hecate is a piece of cake."

"*I'm* not a witch," Jacinth warned darkly.

Mark laughed and pulled her close. The trees were tall here, the path narrow and dim. "I'm not so sure about that," he said. "I have to confess, I'm spellbound. Your eyes have gone sea-blue. How do you do that?"

"They're always changing colour."

"A witch," he said. "I knew it all along. I bet you and Hecate were familiars in an earlier life."

Jacinth laughed, and he kissed her laughing mouth, and when she stopped laughing, kissed her again and then took her hand as they emerged into the sunlight.

Next Month's Romances

Each month you can choose from a wide variety of romance with
Mills & Boon. Below are the new titles to look out for next month
why not ask either Mills & Boon Reader Service or you
Newsagent to reserve you a copy of the titles you want to buy –
just tick the titles you would like and either post to Reader Service
or take it to any Newsagent and ask them to order your books.

Please save me the following titles:	Please tick	✓
ENEMY WITHIN	Amanda Browning	
THE COLOUR OF MIDNIGHT	Robyn Donald	
VAMPIRE LOVER	Charlotte Lamb	
STRANGE INTIMACY	Anne Mather	
SUMMER OF THE STORM	Catherine George	
ICE AT HEART	Sophie Weston	
OUTBACK TEMPTATION	Valerie Parv	
DIVIDED BY LOVE	Kathryn Ross	
DARK SIDE OF THE ISLAND	Edwina Shore	
IN THE HEAT OF PASSION	Sara Wood	
SHADOW OF A TIGER	Jane Donnelly	
BEWARE A LOVER'S LIE	Stephanie Howard	
PASSIONATE OBSESSION	Christine Greig	
SWEET MADNESS	Sharon Kendrick	
STRANGER AT THE WEDDING	Joan Mary Hart	
VALERIE	Debbie Macomber	
OBLIGATION TO LOVE	Catherine O'Connor	

If you would like to order these books in addition to your regular
subscription from Mills & Boon Reader Service please send £1.9
per title to: Mills & Boon Reader Service, Freepost, P.O. Box 236
Croydon, Surrey, CR9 9EL, quote your Subscribe
No:.................................. (If applicable) and complete the name and
address details below. Alternatively, these books are available from
many local Newsagents including W H Smith, J Menzies, Martin
and other paperback stockists from 10 June 1994.

Name:..

Address:...

....Post Code:.........................

**To Retailer: If you would like to stock M&B books pleas
contact your regular book/magazine wholesaler for details.**

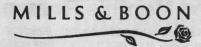

MILLS & BOON

Proudly present...

CHARLOTTE LAMB'S
• 100th •
ROMANCE

This is a remarkable achievement for a writer who had her first Mills & Boon novel published in 1973. Some six million words later and with sales around the world, her novels continue to be popular with romance fans everywhere.

Her centenary romance '*VAMPIRE LOVER*' is a suspense-filled story of dark desires and tangled emotions—Charlotte Lamb at her very best.

Published: June 1994   Price: £1.90

Available from WH Smith, John Menzies, Volume One, Forbuoys, Martins, Woolworths, Tesco, Asda, Safeway and other paperback stockists. Also available from Mills & Boon Reader Service, FREEPOST, PO Box 236, Croydon, Surrey CR9 9EL (UK Postage & Packing free).

Accept 4 FREE Romances and 2 FREE gifts

FROM READER SERVICE

Here's an irresistible invitation from Mills & Boon. Please accept our offer of 4 FREE Romances, a CUDDLY TEDDY and a special MYSTERY GIFT! Then, if you choose, go on to enjoy 6 captivating Romances every month for just £1.90 each, postage and packing FREE. Plus our FREE Newsletter with author news, competitions and much more.

Send the coupon below to:
Mills & Boon Reader Service,
FREEPOST, PO Box 236,
Croydon, Surrey CR9 9EL.

NO STAMP REQUIRED

Yes! Please rush me 4 FREE Romances and 2 FREE gifts! Please also reserve me a Reader Service subscription. If I decide to subscribe I can look forward to receiving 6 brand new Romances for just £11.40 each month, post and packing FREE. If I decide not to subscribe I shall write to you within 10 days - I can keep the free books and gifts whatever I choose. I may cancel or suspend m subscription at any time. I am over 18 years of age.

Ms/Mrs/Miss/Mr _____ EP70

Address _____

_____

Postcode _____ Signature _____